K9 AND COMPANY

'K9, I don't understand. Why are you here? Where are you from?'

'From the Doctor.'

Even then Sarah Jane didn't comprehend. The last thing in her mind was her galactic hero of three years ago. She found herself repeating, 'From the Doctor?'

'Affirmative,' said K9.

And then it all came together for her. With shining eyes and a fast-beating heart the joy tumbled from her in a shout. 'You can't mean the Doctor!'

'My precise meaning, Mistress,' said K9 imperturbably. 'A gift to you.'

Also by Terence Dudley:

Doctor Who – Black Orchid
Doctor Who – The King's Demons

THE COMPANIONS OF DOCTOR WHO

K9 AND COMPANY

Based on the BBC television series by Terence Dudley by arrangement with BBC Books, a division of BBC Enterprises Ltd

TERENCE DUDLEY

A TARGET BOOK
published by
the Paperback Division of
W. H. ALLEN & Co. Plc

A Target Book
Published in 1987
By the Paperback Division of
W. H. Allen & Co. Plc
44 Hill Street, London W1X 8LB

Novelisation copyright © Terence Dudley, 1987
Original script copyright © Terence Dudley, 1981
and 'K9 and Company'
'Doctor Who' series copyright © British Broadcasting Corporation,
1981, 1987

The BBC producer of *K9 and Company* was John Nathan-Turner,
the director was John Black

Printed and bound in Great Britain by
Anchor Brendon Ltd, Tiptree, Essex

ISBN 0 426 20309 7

Contents

Prologue

The full moon hung huge and heavy above the smudging, scurrying November clouds, casting baleful light on the rolling Dorset countryside; a light insufficient for the needs of the inhuman shapes populating the thicket glade. Four guttering tar torches, plunged into the ground at the points of the compass, spluttered sparks in the light wind and threw leaping shadows at the fringing trees: shadows of the thirteen black-cloaked figures standing within a large double circle formed by white stones and slashed by a pentacle, a five-pointed star which followed a continuous line.

Placed at the centre of the magic circle was an oblong wooden block. It served as an altar upon which rested ritualistic artefacts. Illuminated by the fast-shifting flames of two black candles were a rampant horn holding a bunch of herbs, a many-thonged leather scourge, a censer of incense, a small bowl of water and one containing salt, a hazel wand, a long black-handled knife, a tangled length of thick hempen cord, a chalice of red wine and thirteen small, crescent-shaped cakes.

Two of the figures, positioned at either side of the altar, were dramatically distinguishable from their fellows wearing, as they did, great grotesquely exaggerated goat masks. Long gleaming horns thrust at the watching moon, and between them was a single black candle, its flame pulling fiercely at the wick. Beneath the horns the masks plunged to end in a plume of obscene hair. Large, extended ears flanked two macabre voids in which lurked anonymous human eyes.

The smaller of the goat figures bent over the altar. The black-handled knife and the cord were plucked up and offered to the moon, the sleeves of the enveloping cloak falling back to expose slender anomalous female arms. The

High Priestess stood thus for a moment and then turned to face the east.

Hissing as if in acknowledgment of the salutation, the torch drenched the goat mask in ochrous light which penetrated the penumbrous voids to reveal fanatical eyes. The mask-muffled voice intoned fervently as the High Priestess faced south, west and north in turn.

'I summon, stir, and call ye up, ye mighty ones of Air, Fire, Water and Earth, to witness the Rites and to guard the Circle.'

The incantation finished, the High Priestess replaced the knife and the cord on the altar and stood back facing the majestic immobility of the High Priest. It was a signal for two of the black-cloaked coven to move to the altar and lift it clear of the circle exposing a neatly-laid fire beneath an iron grid. A third member of the coven flowed forward and a taper was offered to the southern torch. The figure was tall and the stoop to obtain the light twitched back the cowl of the cloak. The flames twisted the cadaverous face of a man of forty with fierce intelligent eyes glowing below an abundance of dark hair. George Tracey moved smoothly with the lighted taper to the incendiary pile and thrust the flame like a sword into its bowels. The carefully prepared tinder gasped and a moment later the contained blaze was all consuming.

Tracey stood back from the fire and the two who had removed the altar now returned to within the circle, painfully bearing a large iron cauldron whose contents slopped about heavily. The bearers looked at each other over their dangerous burden, both enjoining extreme caution in the other lest the cauldron's volatile contents ignite too soon.

Henry Tobias fought to keep the cauldron's lip level as it was eased above the wind-fanned fire. At fifty he was overweight, the broken capillaries on his cheeks and nose testifying to an indulgent dependence on alcohol. Despite the chill night air beads of sweat were visible through his thinning hair and his small eyes were opaque with barely suppressed panic. His partner's steady, wide-apart eyes were watchful over the rim of the cauldron. Vince Wilson, whose thirty-five years and broad shoulders were taking most of the

8

strain, regretted the coven couldn't be naked to release more cosmic force – to increase bodily strength – but the weather and the nature of the esbat ceremony prohibited this. He offered up a private prayer to Hecate and tightened the muscles of his jaw which had the effect of deepening the crease above the bridge of his nose.

Slowly the cauldron was settled into position and Tobias and Wilson rejoined Tracey at their places within the coven. The statue-like figure of the High Priest came to life with his first move in the ritual. His right hand extended to the High Priestess offering a wood bowl which was taken and held high to the staring moon.

At the edge of the clearing beyond the reach of the torches' feverish fingers where greedy vegetation had overrun what remained of a stone-built ruin, fronds of sere bracken trembled a little before parting to reveal to the moon a pale, taut face. Peter Tracey closely resembled his father, the same dark abundant hair, the same bright, intelligent eyes intent now on the ceremony with neither curiosity nor fear.

The High Priestess held the bowl in front of her, picking from it one by one leaves that she tossed into the smoking cauldron with ceremonious reverence; oak, ash, elm, beech, deciduous leaf followed deciduous leaf into the Cauldron of Regeneration. Soon, the bowl empty, she returned it to the High Priest in exchange for a taper lighted at the southern torch which was held up to the pervading moonlight before being flicked into the cauldron. The vessel roared as the paraffin belched to the height of the enclosing trees signalling the coven to begin its chant of, 'Hecate, Hecate, Hecate . . .' and the slow anti-clockwise dance within the magic circle.

The High Priestess, with slow deliberation, turned again to her male counterpart from whose cloak there appeared, as if by magic, a large, glossy portrait photograph of a strikingly handsome woman in middle age whose lips formed a knowing smile below merry eyes. The portrait was offered to the blank face of the moon before being flicked into the cauldron. Immediately the chanting surged to a crescendo and the dance quickened to become frenetic. When the last trace of the photograph had been consumed by the cauldron

9

the High Priestess flung her arms high, arresting the chant and the dance. Incongruously, from beyond the obscene goat mask there issued a chilling incantation.

'For I speak with the voice of Hecate, your gracious Goddess. I give joy on Earth, certainty not faith while in life, and upon death peace unutterable. To know, to dare, to will, to be silent.'

Peter Tracey shivered at the threat contained in the last heavily accented word. Hands in pockets, he hugged the anorak closer as he moved stealthily into the safe dark beyond the crumbling wall.

1

Exit Aunt Lavinia

Doctor Lavinia Smith was a strikingly handsome woman and, undoubtedly, middle-aged. But the merry eyes and the knowing smile fixed in the photograph printed in the newspaper lying open on the sofa were absent from the face of the woman at the telephone. Lavinia was worried. She listened to the ringing tone having given up all hope that her call would be answered, but powerless to do anything else. She hung up the handset.

'Still not there.'

She moved restlessly to the mullioned seventeenth-century windows to look sightlessly out at the neat garden and the lush green of the undulating Dorset countryside where on the knolls the tufted leafless thickets beckoned the hurrying clouds. 'I should have liked to talk to her before I go.'

'What's the rush?'

The woman on the sofa crossed slim and elegantly sheathed legs. In her late thirties Juno Baker was blessed with a dark, ageless beauty with more than a hint of the voluptuary flowing from her well-poised head to the tips of her Gucci shoes. 'I thought you weren't going until after Christmas.' She prodded the copy of the *North Dorset Echo* lying beside her on the sofa. 'That's what it says here.'

'They want me a month earlier.' Lavinia drifted from the windows to the spitting wood fire. The graceful Jacobean interior reflected the scientist's personality, being functional rather than decorative, but it was comfortable for all that. It was warmly dominated by book-lined walls although there were now gaps on the shelves giving significance to the tea-chest and packing-case lying together near the wide door. 'One of their other lecturers has gone sick.'

Juno's full lips curved in a slow, secret smile. 'That's not what they're saying in the village.'

The merriness danced back into Lavinia's eyes. 'Oh? Why does Hazelbury Abbas think I'm off?'

Before Juno could answer there came two sharp taps on the sitting-room door.

'Yes, come in!' called Lavinia.

The door was opened and two overalled removal men entered with a familiarity tempered by professional discretion. Wordlessly the men took up the tea-chest and hefted it from the room. The door closed quietly after them.

'Well?' asked Lavinia.

'I heard that woman in the Post Office . . . what's her name? Grigson?'

'Gregson.'

'That's what I said.'

Lavinia's merry smile widened. 'Go on!'

'I heard her telling someone that you were being spirited away.'

'Spirited away?' echoed Lavinia incredulously.

'That's what she said. My guess is, Lavinia dear, there's been a reaction to that letter you wrote to the *Echo*.' Juno stabbed at the newspaper with a slim, pink-tipped finger; at the part which carried the picture of Lavinia with the caption, 'Local scientist to tour America.'

'Which letter?' asked Lavinia.

'The one about witchcraft.'

Lavinia blew out her cheeks and her expelled breath fluttered her lips derisively. 'Oh, that. It had to be said. I'm a scientist, Juno. All right, I'm an anthropologist and witchcraft has an important place in my discipline. But I can't be expected to take it seriously . . . not in this day and age . . . particularly when it's on my own doorstep.'

'All right for some,' said Juno briskly. 'They're very superstitious in these parts. There are people here who believe there's been a witches' coven in Hazelbury Abbas since the time this house was built.'

'Poppycock!'

'*You* can afford to be outspoken. And, in any case, you're a

12

comparative newcomer. But it's a bit different for us. We've been here for years but we're still thought of as foreigners. We have to tread gently. If we were to knock the local folklore it'd be taken as criticisms of Hazelbury Abbas itself. And Howard has his work cut out keeping his farm hands as it is. The towns beckon them and Yeovil's no distance.'

Lavinia snorted, not unhappily. 'Silicon chips with everything.'

'That's about the size of it. Try telling the locals about computers. It's easier to believe in witchcraft.'

Lavinia, still restless, stirred the fire unnecessarily and plonked on another log, spraying sparks up into the noble chimney-breast. The other woman watched the activity thoughtfully. 'Is Bill Pollock pleased you're going?'

Lavinia looked round sharply, the poker still in her hand. 'Why should he be?'

'Gives him a free hand with the business, doesn't it?'

Lavinia began twitching the poker unconsciously. 'Bill may be part owner but he doesn't run the place. He does all right on the selling side but it's George Tracey who runs the market garden.'

Juno shuddered. 'That man gives me the creeps.'

'George?' confirmed Lavinia with amusement. 'George is all right. Very clever man.'

'You got any plans for that?'

'What?'

Juno nodded at the poker in Lavinia's hand. 'That. I thought you were conducting an orchestra or thinking of braining me with it.'

Lavinia laughed shortly. 'Still thinking of that girl,' she said, putting down the poker and moving once more to her desk. 'You'd think I'd be used to it by now.'

Sarah Jane Smith's many adventures with the Doctor from the planet Gallifrey were unknown to her aunt. As far as the dedicated scientist knew, her niece's long, mysterious absences were directly attributable to the demands of her itinerant profession, journeying to the four corners of the earth to jot down picaresque nonsenses for newspapers and magazines. If that sort of life made the girl happy she was

13

welcome to it. Although it was a pity she wasn't more communicative. A postcard from time to time wouldn't be unwelcome and this sudden change of plan for her lecture tour could cause complication where Brendan was concerned. She was about to lift the handset of the telephone when she was distracted by another discreet double tap on the door.

'Come in!'

This time the removal men made for the packing-case. Lavinia picked up her handbag from the desk and joined them. 'No, leave that, please. That's not to go.' She rummaged tantalisingly in her bag and the men exchanged a glance. Even very important women scientists were not unfeminine it seemed. Lavinia handed them a generous tip. 'That's it. You've got the lot now.' The men mumbled their thanks, bade her goodbye and left unobtrusively. Lavinia pointed at the packing-case on which was stamped, *For the attention of S. J. S.* She puffed out a long-suffering sigh.

'That's typical of my niece. Delivered to her so long ago I can't remember. I had to bring it with me when I came here. I've told her about it often enough, but she's like a butterfly. Never in one place long enough to lick a stamp.'

'Well, I suppose that's journalism,' comforted Juno. 'What d'you think can be in it?'

'She's never wanted to do anything else.'

'No. I mean what's in the case?'

'Oh! I've no idea.'

'Aren't you curious?'

'I save my curiosity for my work.'

'Oh, Lavinia,' expostulated Juno, 'how pompous!'

Lavinia had to smile at herself. Yes, it was pompous, but the case only served to remind her of her elusive, infuriating, globe-trotting niece. 'I'm sorry,' she said. 'I'm a bit wound up. I don't like loose ends. If only I knew where to reach her it would help.'

Juno picked up her cup of coffee. 'When's she due here?'

'Last Friday.'

'You're worried about your nephew.'

Puzzlement chased the preoccupied look from Lavinia's face. Her mind had been on scheduled airline flights in the antipodes, ponderous camels crossing the Gobi desert, slow boats to China. She looked blankly at Juno who delayed a sip at her cup.

'Brendan, is it?'

Lavinia's mind surfaced from deep sea diving in the Indian Ocean. 'Brendan's my ward.'

'Oh,' said Juno sipping her coffee and thinking that scientists, by definition, must spend their time splitting hairs. 'When does he break up?'

'Next Friday.'

Juno looked at her friend's troubled face and put down her cup briskly but neatly. 'Well, stop looking so anxious!' she commanded. 'He can always come to me, you know. He can muck in with my lot.'

Lavinia's anxiety was eased by the warmth of her gratitude. 'It's sweet of you, Juno, but that's all settled. I rang him yesterday. He'll stay at the school until Sarah Jane collects him.'

Juno chuckled. 'By the look of you you're thinking he may be eligible for a pension by then. Sarah Jane must be quite a girl. I'm looking forward to meeting her.'

'You'll like her,' said Lavinia with enthusiasm. 'But we have one thing in common.'

'What's that?'

'We speak our minds. Loudly.'

2

Enter Sarah Jane

Sarah Jane Smith was doing just that. 'Fool! Idiot! Imbecile! Cretin!'

She sat squirming with frustration behind the wheel of her MGB, the engine growling impatiently. She glanced in the rear mirror, a tight grimace marring her pretty face. The traffic was as bad behind as it was in front. Solid. As if it wasn't bad enough that she was a fortnight overdue. It was beastly unfair. Her assignment had been to cover the famine in Ethiopia not infiltrate rebel forces, as they thought. She didn't wish anybody any harm, particularly one week before Christmas, but how would that silly old trout, shilly-shallying in the car in front, like to spend practically two weeks held incommunicado in a stinking North African military outpost? She wouldn't, would she? So why couldn't she make up her stupid mind?

Sarah Jane had made good headway from the airport after unsuccessfully attempting to telephone Hazelbury Abbas to announce her arrival. She even abandoned all idea of calling first at her south London flat. A first rate driver, she'd enjoyed the challenge offered by eighty miles of the A30 with its heavy, slow-moving goods traffic, overtaking like a wasp or alternatively tucking the car carefully into gaps in front. And now this. A solid traffic jam at Sherborne, five miles from her destination. It wasn't fair. Why did so many people leave their Christmas shopping until the last minute? Silly, when most shops began advertising the festive season in September.

Sarah Jane shivered in her lined leather jacket. The cockpit of the MGB had been enjoyable when exercising her active skills but this enforced passivity only drew attention to the dramatic drop in temperature she'd experienced in the last few hours. She tightened her long woollen scarf and pulled her knitted cap nearer her suffering ears. She'd decided to nip off to the left before the traffic lights ahead, obviously the nub of the obstruction. She'd avoid Cheap Street, the narrow one-way high street that was bound to be thronged with shoppers and choked by delivery vans, and drop down to the station. From there it should be easy to get to the Dorchester Road and then over to Thornford. But the car in front was baulking this plan. Its driver was signalling a right turn manually with her silly arm stuck straight out like a set-square while her near-side-rear indicator light winked wickedly at Sarah Jane's impatience. Oncoming traffic from time to time presented reasonable opportunities for the woman in front to make her turn but she was obviously afflicted by the motorist's most dangerous ailment, timidity. She had also progressively reduced the gap between the rear of her car and the front of the MGB by falling back from non-use of the handbrake, making it impossible for the MGB to turn left.

'Women drivers!' fumed Sarah Jane to herself.

She looked over her shoulder at the man in the car behind who lifted his hands in a gesture of helplessness since the cars behind him were nose to tail making it impossible for him to back up and give room. Sarah Jane looked with fury at the stretch of road in front, now clear of traffic, and did something she had never done before in her young life. She rammed a hand on her horn and held it there. The driver in front jumped and her car performed a series of leaps forward being in first gear with a slipped clutch. Sarah Jane grunted in triumph, went into gear and sped off to the left, throwing a vengeful glance at the timid driver as she did so. Sarah Jane's woman driver looked round reproachfully (having overshot the right turn) presenting a full white beard that matched the flowing locks. Sarah Jane scoffed and then laughed out loud at proof of the irrationality of prejudice.

Leaving Sherborne the MGB purred west along the Yeo Valley, through a vast saucer of mist rising from the river, and entered the village of Hazelbury Abbas from the east. It was some time since Sarah Jane's last visit but she was

17

conscious of no change. The very nature of this part of England resisted the inexorable march or urbanisation, of industrial development encouraged by the thrusting motorways in other areas. Here was nurtured a natural rebellion against the tyranny of time. Here the villagers were content with the richness of their history, the depth of immemorial traditions. All invaders had become restive and retreated as had the Romans.

Sarah Jane drove slowly past the Saxon church with a long, refreshing look at its simple beauty, past the tiny grocery store with its even tinier sub post office, past the compact school building, past the peaceful thatch of the cottages in North Street, past the old water mill to turn into the lichen clothed gates of Bradleigh Manor. As the MGB was nosed along the wide drive to the house Sarah Jane looked beyond it towards the expanse of market garden and the greenhouses that provided her aunt with an income. There seemed to be no activity. Only to be expected, she thought, at this time of year. And yet the house itself looked deserted, like a shunned ghost in the fading afternoon light, with the arched front door and mullioned windows tight shut like closed eyes.

Sarah Jane pressed the doorbell with foreboding, not expecting it to be answered. She pressed the bell again. Where was everybody? It had taken her over two hours to drive from the airport where she'd telephoned and still there was nobody here. Aunt Lavinia and Brendan out doing Christmas shopping? That wasn't the least like her aunt. A voice behind her made her jump.

'Miss Smith?'

Sarah Jane resisted the impulse to face her questioner quickly. She'd learned that to betray one's fear put one at a disadvantage. She faced about slowly only to repress an instinctive shiver. This man had appeared from nowhere without a sound. He was tall and gaunt, about forty years old with piercing eyes and abundant black hair. He was dressed in working clothes, a man of the soil. She kept the tremor from her answer.

'Yes.'

'I've been expecting you. I'm Tracey . . . George Tracey

18

. . . I work for Doctor Smith.'

There was no way for Sarah Jane to know that she was face to face with a witch, a member of the coven that had celebrated the esbat at the last full moon. She felt the adrenalin prickle and became impatient with herself. She'd met more frightening characters than this. What's the matter with you, girl? All that time with the Doctor? Pull yourself together!

'Is my aunt not here?'

Tracey's eyes were intent, unwavering, unblinking. 'She's in America.'

'But she wasn't due to go until after Christmas.'

'She went last Sunday week.'

Why did this man's eyes bother her so? Was it because she feared they were reading her thoughts?

'My aunt wouldn't go without letting me know.'

'I think she wrote to you.'

'I haven't been home. I was delayed abroad. I came straight here.' Why am I being so silly, she thought, and making this sound like a confession?

'There was something about a cable,' said Tracey. His penetrating eyes flicked away for a moment and then flicked back. 'To Reuters?'

'That's who I work for.' Sarah Jane was visited by another fear. 'Isn't Brendan here?'

'Brendan?'

'Brendan Richards. My aunt's ward.'

'There's no one here, miss.'

Where was Brendan? If he wasn't here there was nowhere else for him to go, so far as she knew. Could he be still at school? She watched, alert, as the man suddenly put a hand into his jacket pocket. Tracey held out a bunch of keys. 'Well, anyway, welcome to Bradleigh Manor. These are the keys. That one's for here . . . the front door. The others have tags on. If you want anything you'll find me in the cottage by the farm shop at the back.'

Well, that's friendly enough, thought Sarah Jane. She took the keys. 'Thanks very much.'

'My pleasure,' said Tracey joylessly and crunched his way

19

from the drive towards the distant greenhouses. Sarah Jane looked at the ivy-clad house. The gravel drive extended the length of its front elevation and yet she'd not heard Tracey as he came up behind her. Strange. It was more than strange. It was frightening. Had she been dreaming, preoccupied by the implications of an unexpectedly deserted house? She turned to look at the departing Tracey, shrugged and went to the car for her capacious holdall.

As she let herself into the empty house her anxiety dwelt on Brendan, wherever he was. The arrangement had been that the three of them would spend Christmas together but now it appeared that she was in sole charge of a fourteen-year-old boy with an appetite not only for food but for endless recreation. And she, with a month's leave from her agency, had got herself a commission from *Harper's* for a feature on the revival of English village life. Some hopes. She would be the one in need of revival. Even so, she had to ring the school. Why couldn't he have gone to Sherborne? Why had the boy been sent to school in Berkshire?

She closed the massive front door behind her and crossed the lofty, oak-panelled hall. Leaving her holdall at the foot of the self-important staircase she opened the door of the sitting-room favoured by her aunt; the one she had made into her study. The room was untidy with an air of neglect about it. Unusual for her aunt. She must have left in something of a hurry. The fire grate was empty of everything but abandoned ash. On the table behind the sofa was a tray in charge of a forlorn coffee pot and a lonely cup and saucer. Another cup and saucer looked even more isolated on the desk. Sarah Jane picked up the open newspaper from the sofa and glanced at the photograph of Doctor Lavinia Smith and the item which announced her imminent lecture tour of the United States. She sighed, dropped the newspaper and went to the desk.

The book by the telephone yielded the school's number right enough but neglected to give an alternative number should the first be engaged. She dialled a London number. Listening to the ringing tone her eyes wandered the room and were jerked to the packing-case in its place by the door, overlooked by her when she came in. She was about to abandon the call in favour of satisfying her curiosity when the ringing tone was interrupted by a bright female voice, a little out of breath.

'Hello?'

'Ann. Sarah.'

'Where are you?'

'I'm at Hazelbury Abbas. I had to come straight here.'

'Why? What's wrong?'

'Oh, I got mixed up in some army manoeuvres.'

'You lead a great life.'

'Yes, great if you don't weaken. Listen, have you been in my pad recently?'

'Went in this morning.'

'Any mail?'

'A heap.'

'Would you be a love and forward it?'

'Sure.'

'Thanks. Is there a cable?'

'No.'

'A letter from my aunt. It'll be post-marked here.'

After a short pause the bright, distant, still out of breath voice answered, 'No.'

'Oh!'

'You all right? You sound odd.'

'Do I? No, I'm fine. I've just been taken a little by surprise, that's all. My aunt's shot off to America. I'll bell you some-time. I've got to get Brendan from school. I hope.'

Untypical lack of communication from her aunt had com-pounded Sarah Jane's anxiety. She was about to hang up hurriedly without a valediction when the bright voice at the other end tinkled, 'Merry Christmas!'

'Yes,' gasped Sarah Jane contritely, 'merry Christmas.' She broke the connection quickly and dialled three numbers and was surprised and delighted when the operator re-sponded almost immediately. 'International, please.' This time she wasn't so lucky and her eyes drifted again to the packing-case. Dr Lavinia Smith must have been in an almighty hurry to forget that.

'International. Can I help you?'

'Yes. This is Hazelbury Abbas 778. Could you tell me if a cable has been sent from this number during the last two weeks?'

'I'll check for you and ring you back.'

'Thank you.'

Sarah Jane replaced the handset and bore down on the packing-case. Tucked under one of the two battens reinforcing the top was an envelope addressed *Sarah Jane* in her aunt's handwriting. Sarah Jane snatched it up and fumbled it open with agitated fingers. A short note on a single sheet of writing paper: *It's to be hoped, dear, that you will at last find a feverish moment to open this. It was crammed into the attic at Croydon for years and I've just disinterred it again here. In haste, Aunt Lavinia.*

Short and sweet. Typical of Auntie. No help, but what the Dickens was it? She was going to have to wait to find out, for conjecture about where she could lay hands on a screwdriver or something was interrupted by the shrilling of the telephone. The operator reported that no cable had been sent from Hazelbury Abbas 778 for three months. So much for that. Sarah Jane twitched in her jacket and rubbed her hands together. She was cold. That the central heating was off and the grate empty accounted only for part of the chill in the room. Something was wrong. All right, there was enough evidence that Aunt Lavinia had been in a hurry but she was by disposition and training a neat, methodical woman who was never harrassed. Sarah Jane couldn't understand why something a little warmer than the bleak Tracey and a bunch of keys hadn't been arranged for her arrival.

She was startled by the jangling of the front door bell agitated by a cable attached to a worn knob at the outer wall; a method of summons by a caller that had withstood the implacable advance of electricity. It bothered Sarah Jane that the sound had made her jump. What on earth was the matter with her?

The figure outside was silhouetted in the thickening afternoon light.

'Hello! I'm Peter Tracey. My Dad sent me over. He thought you might be able to use this.' He thrust out an arm

22

and Sarah Jane could have kicked herself for flinching as she accepted the thermos flask. 'Cup of tea.'

She could see now that he looked very like his father in spite of the smile that softened his face. She relaxed. Such an act could only mean that she wasn't as unwelcome as she had been made to feel by the older man.

'How very kind,' she said. 'Thank you, Peter, and please thank your father for me.'

'You're welcome,' said the young man shyly and turned and retreated as his father had done, half twisting about as he heard the telephone begin to ring in the house.

Sarah Jane closed the front door and hurried back into the sitting-room, snatching up the handset. 'Yes?' She listened to the distant bleeps until they were stilled by a clattering coin.

'Sarah?' The voice at the other end was small and plaintive.

'Who's that?'

'Brendan.'

'Brendan! I was just going to ring you. I'm sorry. I got held up and I've only just arrived. It's a bit late now. I'll come for you tomorrow morning.' Sarah Jane had had enough travelling for one day. It wouldn't hurt the boy to stay at school for one more night.

'If you do I'll be frozen solid.'

'What?'

'I'm in a phone box at the station.'

'What station?'

'Sherborne.'

Brendan Richards had darted into the solitary telephone box outside the ticket office anxious to be taken home. He'd scuttled into the box ahead of a slower moving fat man without realising that they had a common destination until, with the handset to his ear, he'd turned to see the portly gent now at the head of a small queue all no doubt thinking that the youth of today was entirely without manners or respect for elders. He was unrepentant. He'd watched all the other boys in his house go scooting off home for Christmas hols with the exception of that deadly bore Jarvis whose parents were in New Guinea or something silly. He'd felt lonely and isolated

23

for the better part of a fortnight and he'd had enough. There was bound to be someone at home. If not, he'd walk. 'Sarah?'

Sarah Jane was breathing hard. The boy had been told to stay at school until fetched. What on earth was he doing at Sherborne station?

'What's the idea?'

'I got fed up waiting.'

'Oh, you got fed up waiting.' She couldn't keep the sarcasm out of her voice. Fourteen years old and he'd got fed up waiting. She'd been held, practically at gunpoint, in a squalid Ethiopian village while he was being pampered by an underemployed matron at school and he'd got fed up waiting. Tough! Her tone wasn't wasted on Brendan.

'I'd take a taxi but I haven't got enough money.'

Sarah Jane was immediately contrite. 'No, no,' she said hastily, 'I'm on my way.'

3

An Invitation

Sarah Jane was quite looking forward to her reunion with Brendan. It was some time since she'd seen him and he was a likeable lad; mature for his age without being precocious even if he did, she remembered, having a marked predilection for terrible schoolboy jokes involving a lot of noise and graphic antics. She favoured a gentler, more economic humour.

The Manor was a matter of five miles from Sherborne and Sarah Jane, who never hung about on four wheels, wasn't long getting to the station where the woman who had been second in the telephone queue was still feeding ten pence coins into the voracious talking machine. The red MGB snarled up and stopped level with Brendan waiting by his suitcase on the pavement.

'OK, hop in!' cooed Sarah Jane. 'Bung that in the back!'

But Brendan had eyes only for the sports car as he tucked himself into the passenger seat. 'I say! What about this! Ace!' he enthused.

'Nice to see you again, Brendan,' said Sarah Jane energetically.

'What?' muttered Brendan uncomprehendingly, deflected from his examination of the ace roadster. Sarah Jane leaned over and kissed him lightly on the cheek with a sudden gush of affection released by the boy's total ingenuousness.

'Oh! Yes!' responded Brendan, recalling that another human being occupied the dream car. 'Yes, nice to see you, Sarah. Can I drive it?'

Sarah Jane sighed. Fourteen years old, at one of the best schools in the country, and still his grammar was grubby.

'Do you mean are you able to drive it or may you drive it?'

'Oh, I'm able to drive it, all right,' replied Brendan

innocently.

'You can drive?'

'Of course.'

'Of course at fourteen?'

'Travis could drive when he was thirteen.'

'Who's Travis?'

'Chap who taught me . . . in the summer. Tractor on his father's farm.'

Sarah Jane blinked. And there was she thinking he wasn't precocious. 'This isn't a tractor,' she said tartly.

'No, it's fantastic. How long have you had it?'

'About a year.'

'Fantastic! When we get home can I take it up the drive?'

'You mean *may* you take it up the drive.'

'Yes.'

'No.'

'Oh! Why not?'

The disappointment on the boy's face was more bitter than the winter wind that hissed in her face round the windscreen. How could she tell him that she didn't want the gears ground, the clutch slipped or the engine overrevved, all the inevitable crimes committed by the beginner?

'I'll think about it,' she said going into gear and shooting smoothly off with the firm intention of demonstrating an inimitable performance behind the wheel of her car. Fourth form schoolboys driving sports cars? What next?

'What'll she do?' asked Brendan as they skirted south of the town and headed west.

'Do?' echoed Sarah Jane with misgiving.

'What speed?' persisted the envious Brendan. Sarah Jane was suddenly visited by the fearsome vision of her car, with Brendan at the controls, leaping forward from the gates of the Manor and developing into an eighty miles an hour projectile with them finishing up in the sitting-room without conventional use of the front door and decided to change the subject. 'I'm worried,' she announced.

'Oh,' responded a sympathetic Brendan, still engrossed by the MGB. 'What about?'

'The arrangements for collecting you. What did she say

exactly?'

'Aunt Lavinia?'

Irritation prompted by an unstilled, persistent anxiety provoked Sarah Jane into a display of impatience. 'Who else?'

'Well, you could have meant Matron.'

Touché, thought Sarah Jane, softening immediately. '*When* did Aunt Lavinia phone?'

'Only the day before we broke up. She said I'd have to stay at school until you came for me.'

'Nothing else?'

'No.'

'Nothing about the reason for suddenly going off like that?'

'Only that they wanted her earlier.'

'Just before Christmas?'

Brendan thought for a moment. 'The Americans don't go much on Christmas, do they?'

Sarah Jane had allowed the car to drift into the middle of the road in anticipation of cutting the many bends. She'd forgotten that Dorset was the county of winding roads and lanes, lending infinite variety for the serious driver; the serious driver, that is, whose mind wasn't hopping about between Hazelbury Abbas and the United States of America. She saw the car ahead just in time. The Ford Escort was fifty yards away and closing fast. Its driver braked hard and the car veered dangerously to the left in a violent skid, burning rubber. Sarah Jane knew better. She changed down with swift dexterity and steered the MGB neatly past the Ford whose nearside front wheel was mounted on the grass verge with its driver mounted on the horn.

'Stupid man!' announced Sarah Jane. Brendan reacted to the incident with mixed feelings, his admiration in conflict with the furious tingling going on at the back of his neck. But the stupid man in the Ford, maniacally sounding his horn, was already erased from Sarah Jane's mind which had returned to the other side of the Atlantic in a tithe of the time it had taken her to change gear. 'Very odd,' she muttered. Brendan, however, was still pondering the prospect of death at an extremely early age. 'You were in the middle of the road,' he pointed out with more than a degree of indignation.

'I was thinking about Aunt Lavinia going to America.'

'I see. Where they drive on the right.'

'Watch it, buster,' growled Sarah Jane warningly.

'I can't think what you're worried about,' said Brendan by way of a peace-offering. 'She'll be all right, won't she?'

'How would I know? I've been abroad for the last fortnight.'

'Well, why don't you ring her?' offered Brendan.

'I would if I knew where she was. That's the whole point. Going like that without letting me know or leaving word where she could be reached.'

'Oh,' murmured Brendan helpfully. There was a silence between them until they reached the outskirts of Hazelbury Abbas when a thought occurred to Brendan. 'Are you home for good now?'

'Here? Yes. But I don't know about for good.'

'But you're not dashing off again to do another job somewhere?'

'Not for a bit, no.'

'Great!' exclaimed Brendan. Sarah Jane glanced at him suspiciously. Her relationship with the boy was hardly of long standing since they met but sporadically and she had no reason to believe that he was excessively fond of her or her company.

'What's great about it?'

That penetrating look disquieted Brendan a little. He wanted her as an ally. 'I'm hoping to persuade Aunt Lavinia to let me go to the Comprehensive here.'

'Oh, are you?' So that was it. Two fully extended professional women sharing a house with a schoolboy. Well, one of those women was going to put her foot down. The MGB roared past the church as Sarah Jane fleshed out the metaphor, startling an old lady walking her dog. The foot eased off the throttle as Sarah Jane went on: 'Then you'd better start persuading me. I'm here to write, not be a surrogate mum.'

Brendan was hurt. Why was it that grown-ups had to be so

patronising? 'I'm old enough to look after myself.'

Sarah Jane smiled secretly. What a lot kids took for granted! Cooking, cleaning, washing, ironing, not to mention shopping. Ah, well. Let it be! She contented herself with: 'I thought you liked it at Wellington.'

'I do. I think it's great,' said Brendan, 'But I don't like boarding and Aunt Lavinia's got a better library.' Sarah Jane was disposed to take more kindly to that particular sentiment. If his interest in the books was genuine he certainly wasn't work-shy. 'Developing an interest in anthropology now, are we?'

'Not specially,' said Brendan, 'but I'm thinking of taking three early O levels; maths, chemistry and biology.'

Sarah Jane was impressed, feeling a little ashamed of her earlier unworthy thoughts. 'Why those in particular? Going in for science?'

'I thought I'd have a crack at farming,' declared Brendan. 'I think, on the whole, I'd rather grow things than make things and I certainly don't want to sit in an office all day. I enjoyed it on Travis's farm in the summer. And his father says it's all very scientific these days and getting more so.'

Sarah Jane was doubly impressed with the patent enthusiasm. No, the lad certainly wasn't work-shy.

'Besides,' went on Brendan, 'there's the shooting and the fishing.'

Ah, thought Sarah Jane, the shooting and the fishing. She'd forgotten about that. 'Not to mention the hunting,' she added.

'Oh, they don't hunt,' said Brendan innocently, 'but I got quite good at shooting clay.'

As Sarah Jane turned in at the Manor gates and started up the drive she was reminded of Brendan's feverish interest in taking the wheel of her motor car and was grateful that this enthusiasm had been eclipsed by one even more frenetic. Brendan was still vigorously expounding the niceties of the technique of pulverising clay discs against an uncomplaining sky when Sarah Jane pulled up at the front door of the Manor. Possibly because she was watching for it she immediately noticed a violent conflict of interests reflected on

Brendan's expressive face as memory flooded back. 'No,' she said categorically. .

'No what?' responded a perplexed Brendan.

'No shooting and no driving. You're too young for a licence for either.'

'I never said a word!'

'You didn't have to.'

As Brendan humped his suitcase from the back of the car Sarah Jane approached the front door jangling her newly inherited bunch of keys making a mental note to do something about having to carry around such a vast quantity of metal. She felt like a medieval chatelaine and the house wasn't as old as that. She was taking the heavy key from the lock when she noticed that the hall light was on; something that again stirred anxiety. The house she'd entered earlier couldn't have been more bleak or unwelcoming but now, somehow, the atmosphere was different without improvement. There was something frightening about electric light being turned on in a hitherto empty house. She was about to be even more disturbed.

Brendan was coming through the door behind her when a long, low snarl snatched at her stomach. Through the open sitting-room door bounded a dangerous beast that fetched up in the middle of a Persian carpet as if by some preordained design. The mask of the brutish Alsatian was stretched tightly back from the clenched teeth and anticipatory saliva dribbled onto the carpet.

'Don't move!' whispered Brendan tautly.

'Wasn't going to,' hissed back a terrified Sarah Jane.

'Jasper! Sit!' called an authoritative masculine voice. The salivating savage instantly snapped shut the stretched upper snout, removing the threat from exposed teeth, and turned a lowered head with snivelling servility towards the sitting-room. It fell back obediently on its haunches as a tall, stout man of perhaps sixty-five years came into the hall. He was dressed in a well-cut tweed suit that had seen long service and carried himself with the insouciance of the born leader. Sarah Jane didn't like him. She knew him to be her aunt's partner in the market garden business but it irritated her that she

30

couldn't remember his name. What she did remember was that he was gruff, outspoken and overbearingly sure of himself and lived in a charming seventeenth-century cottage at Yetminster. With the bunch of keys still heavy in her hand she wondered what he was doing here and, for that matter, *how* he was doing here.

'My name's Pollock,' announced Commander William Pollock, Royal Navy, retired. 'I'm your aunt's partner.'

'Yes, we met about two years ago.'

'We did, we did. Briefly. Thought you mightn't remember.'

Sarah Jane was never likely to forget. One of the workers in the market garden shop had been in grave financial trouble and had put a hand in the till. Aunt Lavinia had done her best to persuade Pollock to her lenient view but the Commander would have none of that. He lived and breathed the inflexible moral code set by the Senior Service. The police had been sent for and the unfortunate youth charged. 'Do you know Brendan?' she heard herself saying.

'Brendan?'

'Brendan Richards, Aunt Lavinia's ward.'

Pollock eyed Brendan with disapproval as if to say that he didn't know the boy and didn't much want to. 'How d'you do, boy?'

'How do you do, sir?'

Pollock blinked and the muscles around his mouth relaxed a little. The lad had good manners, he'd say that for him. But then, by all accounts, he went to a good school.

'Broken up, have you?'

'Yes.'

'Long holiday, the Christmas holiday. Know anything about farming . . . horticulture?'

'Not a lot, sir. But during the summer hols I . . .'

But the Commander had heard enough. Not a lot meant more than a little and that, in any young boy's consciousness, meant that he knew it all. He cut in sharply, 'That's all right. We've all a lot to learn. Leave it to me. I'll keep you out of mischief.'

The look that passed between Brendan and Sarah Jane was intercepted by Pollock. The muscles about his mouth relaxed even more to allow a smile that changed completely the man's persona. Sarah Jane saw at once that the gruffness and directness were by no means the whole man. The smile was unforced, open, charming. Suddenly it made a great deal more sense that this was the man her aunt had taken into partnership. 'Forgive the intrusion,' the Commander went on. 'I was told you were here so I thought I'd warm things up a bit for you. Pretty poor welcome, but nobody seemed to know you were coming. I hope you don't mind. I got a fire going.' With an expansive gesture that suited his frame Pollock indicated the sitting-room and Sarah Jane accepted the tacit invitation to precede him into it.

The room had been transformed. A fire danced cheerfully in the grate, the curtains had been drawn to shut out the cold, darkening afternoon, the lamps were warm and welcoming. But there was something else that made the room different in Sarah Jane's eyes; something not immediately apparent that came to her suddenly as she stretched out chilled hands to the warmth of the fire. There was no sign of the newspaper that had announced her aunt's departure to the United States.

Sarah Jane turned to Pollock as he came into the room followed by an overawed Brendan for whom the Commander painfully represented the authoritarian voice of the Chief Petty Officer in the Combined Cadet Force at school. 'Thank you. This is very kind.'

'The least I could do,' responded Pollock. And then, rightly interpreting a cloud on Sarah Jane's otherwise pert face, he anticipated her question. 'I got used to just dropping in when your aunt was here.'

Sarah Jane turned from the fire to put the bunch of keys on the table at the back of the sofa. It was an unvoiced question for which the Commander had a ready answer. 'The back door was open.'

'You live at Yetminster, don't you?'

'Yes, but I'm here most of the time. Your aunt let me have a couple of rooms in the east wing about a year ago. It's better that way with me being on the spot, so to speak.'

The cloud cleared from Sarah Jane's pretty face. That explained Pollock's sudden appearance and the late welcome but there remained the mystery of Aunt Lavinia's abrupt departure without leaving word apart from the curt note on the packing-case which still stood unmoved and unmolested near the door. Sarah Jane remembered her manners. 'Do please,' she began, but her invitation for the Commander to sit down was interrupted by that gentleman making himself comfortably at home on the sofa.

Brendan had wandered over to the packing-case. 'What's this?' he asked.

'I don't know,' replied Sarah Jane. 'It was at the old house in Croydon. Aunt Lavinia brought it here when she moved.'

'It's got *For the attention of S.J.S.* stamped on it.'

'Yes, I know.'

'Well, aren't you curious?'

'Of course I'm curious,' Sarah Jane almost snapped. What was wrong with the boy? Couldn't he see that this was no time for indulging his curiosity about that wretched packing-case?

Jasper loped in from the hall and stood, with lolling tongue, looking expectantly at his master. Pollock glared. 'No,' he growled and pointed a finger at the door. The dog instantly turned and, with wagging tail, trotted out into the hall. The commander smiled after the animal affectionately. 'Man's best friend must know his place,' he said. 'The most endearing trait in a dog is total obedience.'

That just about sums this man up, thought Sarah Jane. Man's best friend. Man's best slave, more like. Power. That must be the motive moving every dog lover, every dog owner. The need to dominate, the need to be in complete control of another animal, the need to boost one's ego, one's self-esteem. Good dog! Good self-gratification! She suddenly felt mean. What about guide dogs for the blind! Here total obedience replaced lost eyes, safeguarded life and limb. 'Yes,' she said aloud. 'Would you like a cup of tea?' She looked across at Brendan who was still inspecting the packing-case. 'Brendan, be a good chap and put a kettle on, will you?'

'No, thank you, m'dear. Not for me,' said Pollock. 'I must be getting about me business.'

As Brendan's attention immediately returned to the packing-case Sarah Jane said: 'But I'd like one.'

Brendan followed Jasper, barely repressing a sigh and Sarah Jane sat down opposite the Commander. 'How *is* the business?'

Pollock grimaced. 'Couldn't be worse. We've had two terrible years. If we don't pick up next year I can see us going bankrupt. We operate on a three year cycle. Everything depends on the weather.'

Sarah Jane's question was prompted more by politeness than curiosity. She knew Aunt Lavinia didn't depend on the market garden for a livelihood, that she'd inherited the place from Uncle Nicholas and looked on it as little more than a hobby, but she was rather surprised to hear that things were not good. She'd known the market garden shop when it was thronged with customers throughout the summer months when Uncle Nicholas was alive. And there were bound to be good years and bad. But then farmers and the like were always complaining. It was longstanding tradition. She remembered those summer weekends when she joined the customers, dotted about the acres of strawberry beds and raspberry canes, picking the seemingly inexhaustible soft fruit.

'Even the soft fruit, the pick-it-yourself side?'

'Everything,' said the Commander gloomily. 'Last spring was wet and warm and that was all right. But the weekends were bad. A fine Saturday in the summer and you can be sure of up to a thousand customers in a day. But bad weather and you can forget it. The year before we had two late frosts. Killed the lot.'

Sarah Jane knew nothing about the art of growing things but there were surely ways of anticipating the weather. 'Nothing under glass?' she asked.

The Commander fidgeted with his irritation. Here was another one who knew it all. 'Only some propagating.' What could this child know about labour difficulties on the land in the midst of a second industrial revolution, the revolution of the silicon chip? 'You can't get the labour for high input, output stuff. Not in this area. On the coast maybe. Not here.'

34

Brendan came back into the room looking satisfied with a crumb or two still clinging to his upper lip which, thought Sarah Jane, were good signs which suggested that he'd succeeded in the major feat of putting on the kettle and had found some biscuits into the bargain. She was feeling peckish. She was also reminded that fostering in Brendan an interest in the activities of the market garden could solve the problem of how to keep the fourteen-year-old entertained and out of her working way. 'Well,' she said, 'I'm sorry to hear all that and, what's more, I'm going to be no help whatsoever.'

'Your aunt rather left it to me,' said Pollock succinctly. 'A sort of sleeping partner.'

Sarah Jane ignored the snub. 'Brendan says farming's all scientific these days.'

'Does he?' The Commander turned a bleak eye on the becrumbed adolescent.

'It's fantastic,' said Brendan, nothing daunted. 'I've a friend at school whose father took us to this fabulous place in Hertfordshire. Rothamsted, it's called, and they do fabulous things there all to do with soil research. Travis says that soon they'll . . .'

'Do they?' cut in Pollock with no change of tone. 'I have friends too. But it's not all a matter of science. It's common sense and experience.' He looked from one to the other pointedly. 'Mostly experience. Your aunt was happy to leave everything to me.'

'Oh, as I shall be,' said Sarah Jane hastily. 'Make no mistake. I have work of my own to do.'

'Capital!' said the Commander with relieved emphasis. The relief was to be short-lived.

'But I don't mind lending a hand,' put in Brendan enthusiastically. 'I'm pretty good at driving a tractor, even if I say so myself.'

'Thank you,' said Pollock dismissively. 'I'll bear it in mind.'

Brendan knew from his tone that he had no such intention and followed up with: 'And, as a matter of fact, I can handle two types. A Ferguson and a Ford. What have you got here?'

'Neither,' said the Commander bluntly.

'I'm sure Brendan wouldn't want to get in the way,' said Sarah Jane placatingly. 'Would you, Brendan?'

'Of course not.'

'Good,' said the Commander getting up, 'then we're all happy.' His mood changed again with his charming smile. 'As happy as possible, at any rate.'

'I'm far from happy about Aunt Lavinia going off like that,' said Sarah Jane. 'Suddenly, without a word. She's never done anything like that before. It's very worrying.'

Pollock looked at her sympathetically. 'She tried hard enough to reach you, I know that. And I'm pretty sure she sent a wire. She told me she was going to, anyway.'

'Not by telephone,' said Sarah Jane heavily. 'I've been on to them.'

'Then I'd check with Lily Gregson at the Post Office. Not much Lily doesn't know . . . about everybody.'

In spite of her concern Sarah Jane was amused by the wicked glint in the Commander's eye. He was telling her that the traditional village gossip was the local sub post mistress. And who could be better placed having, as she did, sight of Hazelbury Abbas's telecommunications? 'I'll do that,' she said.

'Don't look so worried, m'dear! Lavinia's all right. She's a tough one and well able to look after herself.'

'Oh, yes,' agreed Sarah Jane. 'It's just that I can't get rid of the feeling that something's happened to her. If she left when Mr Tracey said she did why hasn't she been in touch? A postcard or something.'

Pollock looked thoughtful, his eyes wandering as he pondered. 'D'you know who her hosts are in the States?'

'That's just it. She's on a lecture tour.'

'She had to start somewhere, didn't she?'

'That's true. But all the arrangements will have been made by her agent and I haven't a clue who that is.'

'Yes. Tricky one,' agreed the Commander. 'If you're that worried you'll just have to go on asking around. Somebody's bound to know, of that you can be certain. I must be off. I'll see myself out.' He eased to the door, a move that brought a

36

happy yelp from Jasper.

'Shut up, you!' barked back Pollock, the dog acknowledging the command with a whimper.

Sarah Jane waved a hand in a gesture which took in the room. 'And many thanks for . . .'

The telephone rang startlingly, cutting her short.

'There,' said Pollock confidently, 'what's the betting that's Lavinia now?' He came back into the room a little as Sarah Jane picked up the handset.

'Hazelbury Abbas double seven eight.'

The voice at the other end was pleasant and pitched low but it wasn't Aunt Lavinia's.

'Miss Smith?'

'Yes.'

'This is Juno Baker, a friend of your aunt's.'

Sarah Jane liked the voice. It was warm and reassuring. 'Hello,' she responded.

'Hello, my dear. I heard you'd arrived. All's well I hope?'

Sarah Jane wanted to say it wasn't but something stopped her. She said, 'Yes, thank you.'

'I wondered if you'd like to come over for a drink a little later. That's if you're not too exhausted.'

If Sarah Jane wasn't exactly exhausted she'd had about enough for one day. On the other hand if this woman was a friend of her aunt's she might have news of her. She stopped herself blurting out the question there and then, not wanting to do so with Pollock still there. His attitude, though comforting, made her feel immature, a little hysterical. 'It's very kind of you,' she began when the voice at the other end overlapped hers.

'You might like to meet some of the locals, and we're only just a bit up the road.'

So it was a party, a seasonal party. One of those stand-up affairs that were the inevitable run-up to Christmas, where you clung to an oft-filled glass and did your best to spot the bores before they spotted you. She could do without that. She said: 'It *is* most kind of you. Would you let me think about it?'

The voice at the other end purred sympathetically. 'Of

course, my dear. Don't feel pressed. Just come if you feel like it. We're at the Lodge. Opposite the church. Any time after half past six.'

'Er . . . thank you,' said Sarah Jane hesitantly. Goodbye.'

Juno Baker replaced the telephone and turned triumphantly to face her husband; a man in his late forties, tall, handsome but inclined to a certain puffiness which spoke of good living if not indulgence.

'She'll come.'

'Good,' said Howard Baker with satisfaction.

4

A Gift from the Doctor

Sarah Jane replaced the handset slowly and thoughtfully and looked at the hovering Pollock. 'Someone called Juno Baker. A friend of my aunt's. Inviting me over.'

The Commander grunted.

'What does that mean?' she asked.

'What?'

Sarah Jane did her best to imitate Pollock's grunt bringing a chuckle from Brendan and a smile of appreciation from the object of her jest.

'It means,' said the Commander, 'that if you take my advice you won't go. Keep away from that lot! Howard Baker's our biggest competitor. He's not only got his twenty-five hundred acres here, he's got an even bigger place at Halstock.'

'Where's that?'

'On the way to Beaminster. He's so big that what he loses on the swings he gains on the roundabouts. We haven't got any roundabouts. I'll leave you to it.'

In the doorway he turned back and pointed to the keys on the table by the sofa. 'And a little more advice. I'm going out the back way, the way I came. Lock the door after me!' And he went out with a 'Heel!' for the benefit of Jasper.

Sarah Jane picked up the bunch of keys and followed. Brendan immediately homed on the mysterious packing-case, patting it, tipping it on edge to assess its weight, looking about for some sort of tool with which to satisfy a, by now, compulsive curiosity. He'd have to ask Sarah first, of course.

Sarah Jane let the Commander and his dog out of the back door and locked it after them. With a grimace at the bunch of keys she made her way to the kitchen by the side of the stairs and got rid of the keys on the table in its centre, a table dwarfed by the old-fashioned room which was clean and tidy with everything in its proper place. She touched the electric kettle which had boiled and switched itself off. She rummaged about, with her mind on Juno Baker, and found a teapot and a caddy. She poured water from the kettle into the pot and then depressed the switch on the kettle to bring the water back to the boil with her mind still on Juno Baker and whether or not she should accept her invitation. A sudden noise behind her twitched her round. It was Brendan.

'Don't care for him much,' he said.

'What?' said Sarah Jane, her mind on the Lodge opposite the church.

'Old Pollock.'

'Oh, he's all right. Though I can't think why he's afraid I'm here to take over. You, on the other hand, are certainly a threat.'

She emptied the teapot and spooned in tea from the caddy. 'I'd take it easy if I were you.'

'All I said was that I could drive a tractor.' Brendan began a systematic examination of the kitchen opening and closing cupboards and drawers.

'What *are* you doing?' asked Sarah Jane.

'Looking for something to open your packing-case with.'

'Oh, are you?'

'Don't you want to know what's in it?'

'Not as much as you do, it seems.'

'Oh, come on, Sarah, don't be so uptight!'

'Uptight! Me?'

'Yes. You.' The kettle burbled to the boil and switched itself off with a sharp click. Sarah Jane jumped. 'See what I mean?'

Sarah Jane relaxed and grinned at herself. 'Oh, shut up!' she said good-naturedly. Brendan chirped with delight as he found what he was looking for. He held up a sturdy-looking screwdriver. 'All right?' he asked.

'Oh, go on then,' said Sarah Jane, pouring water into the teapot. Brendan galloped out of the kitchen and across the hall into the sitting-room. When Sarah Jane followed him in he was already attacking the top of the case with much verve.

She winced at the screeching of complaining nails as the top was wrenched free. The contents of the case were protected by a wrapping of what looked like polystyrene but of a type not seen by either of them before. Brendan's exploring fingers prodded into the material trying to find a hold. He got a good grip and attempted to pull the contents clear without success.

'Whatever it is it's very heavy,' he said.

'Aunt Lavinia says she's had it for ages,' said Sarah Jane. 'Stuck away in the attic at Croydon. You'll never get it out like that. Take the side off!'

'What?'

'Prise the side off! Here, let me.'

'All right, all right, I can do it. Who's not interested?' smirked Brendan. He pushed the screwdriver in at a point between two sides of the case and began to lever out the larger elevation. Protesting noisily the side was pulled off. Still all that was visible was the protective wrapping. Brendan eased the amorphous contents away from what remained of the case and onto the carpet and Sarah Jane began tearing at the thing with impatient fingers. 'Have you ever noticed,' she said with some irritation, 'that nowadays it's a full-time job getting at an increasing number of goods through layers of plastic? Whatever were things covered with before this beastly stuff? Somebody ought to invent a tool to deal with it. They'd make a fortune.'

'What's wrong with this?' asked Brendan wielding the screwdriver enthusiastically.

'Careful!' warned Sarah Jane, 'Whoever packed this considered it to be fragile.'

Brendan picked cautiously at the defiant wrapping until he'd made a sizeable hole and was soon happily tugging the material to shreds. As strip after strip was pulled away it exposed gleaming metal that took progressive shape. What at last lay revealed caused the two to look at each other in amused wonderment.

'Looks just like a dog,' said Brendan. 'A metal dog.'

'How strange,' murmured Sarah Jane. 'Who could be sending me this? Isn't there a message?' They both rummaged in the plastic-strewn ruins of the packing-case.

'Nothing,' said Brendan, and then he suddenly saw something. He pointed at what looked like a small flange on the metal animal's neck. 'Look, a collar with a name tag.'

Sarah Jane bent forward for a close look. 'Nothing on it,' she announced.

'What about that?' wondered Brendan. 'It *is* a dog, isn't it? A sort of mechanical dog.'

'You mean it moves?'

'I don't know. It might.'

Brendan ran his hands methodically over the contraption's easily recognisable features; ears, snout, tail.

'No legs,' remarked Sarah Jane.

Brendan manually examined the omissions in this area. 'No legs,' he confirmed, 'but it's got sort of caterpillar treads. That suggests it works.'

'Works?'

'Well, moves about.'

Sarah Jane studied the mystifying mass of metal with growing irritation. If this was some sort of joke it wasn't at all funny as far as she was concerned. And it was clearly meant for her. She looked again at the part of the ruptured packing-case on which was indelibly stamped, *For the attention of S.J.S.* Not much doubt about that. But what was the thing all about? She thought aloud. 'What's the point?'

'Erm,' grunted Brendan helpfully.

'What's the purpose of it? What's it do?'

'We could try asking it.'

'Chump!' said Sarah Jane easily. She began to prod nervously at the metal dog as if expecting an electric shock.

'It's not going to bite,' grinned Brendan.

'How can you be so sure?' bit back Sarah Jane continuing her cautious exploration.

But then, suddenly, a number of startling thing began to happen, far more surprising than if the thing had threatened Sarah Jane with a set of teeth. There was a low purr as if from a motor and two small lights came on forming eyes. At the same time the tail began to wag. Brendan laughed delightedly. 'What about that?' he cried.

42

'Mistress?' The voice was flat but the inflection was clear, startling Sarah Jane. She glared accusingly at Brendan.

'Don't muck about!' she rapped.

'Don't look at me!' objected Brendan.

'*I* spoke, Mistress.'

Sarah Jane was looking directly at Brendan and his lips hadn't moved. She looked down at the newly-illuminated mechanical dog.

'It speaks,' cried a delirious Brendan. 'It speaks.'

A flabbergasted Sarah Jane looked incredulously at the mechanical talking dog. She couldn't be dreaming. She pinched herself to make sure. Mistress? What could it all mean? She looked at the marvelling Brendan. 'Whatever is it?'

'I am K9, mark three,' said the dog flatly.

'K9, mark three,' echoed Sarah Jane hollowly.

'Affirmative,' said K9.

Brendan squeaked before a series of uncontrollable guffaws took possession of him. He pointed at K9 and tears pushed their way through closed eyelids. He recovered long enough to blurt the two syllables, 'canine,' before surrendering to fresh paroxysms.

Sarah Jane sighed. All right, a joke's a joke, but did he have to make all that noise? Besides she wanted to know where this phenomenol piece of engineering originated and she couldn't think with the boy doing possible injury to his vocal chords. 'Brendan,' she cried, 'stop honking!'

Brendan pulled himself together with considerable effort, wiping the tears from his face and muttering, 'Canine, canine,' to himself. He was quiet for a moment but not long enough for Sarah Jane to put the question dominant in her mind for he erupted into renewed laughter punctuated by attempts to speak. 'D'you think . . .' he began before succumbing to debilitating giggles. 'D'you think you'll need . . .' but he was off again. Sarah Jane stamped her foot and growled. Brendan managed at last to get enough control of his merriment to finish his statement but it came with a rush approximating to a shriek. 'D'you think you'll need a licence?' and he fell about again. Sarah Jane looked at him pityingly. There ought to be a law about schoolboy humour or, at least, a marketable cure for it. 'Brendan,' she said with acerbity, 'shut your silly face!' Brendan did his best to oblige but succeeded only in fixing a wide smile of genuine pleasure on the canine artefact.

'K9,' began Sarah Jane.

'Mistress?' came the response. Brendan giggled.

'Will you shut up, you stupid boy!' shouted Sarah Jane angrily. Brendan lifted his eyes ceilingwards as if to imply that women were woefully lacking a sense of humour and she tried again.

'K9, I don't understand. Why are you here? Where are you from?'

'From the Doctor.'

Even then Sarah Jane didn't comprehend. The last thing in her mind was her galactic hero of three years ago. She found herself repeating, 'From the Doctor?'

'Affirmative,' said K9.

And then it all came together for her. With shining eyes and a fast-beating heart the joy tumbled from her in a shout. 'You can't mean the Doctor!'

'My precise meaning, Mistress,' said K9 imperturbably. 'A gift to you.'

Sarah Jane looked on K9 anew with lachrymal happy eyes. A gift from the Doctor! He hadn't forgotten her. He'd been thinking of her even when she thought he'd blown it all those years ago. Of course! Of course this bizarre mechanical dog, already projecting vital personality, was so typical of the Doctor. How he must have chuckled as he wrapped his gift with such care! She thought aloud: 'Doctor! You didn't forget!'

Having recovered from his laughing fit Brendan was feeling rather left out of things. What was going on here? Sarah and this K9 were actually engaged in a conversation about what appeared to be a mutual friend. Whatever it was that was going on, this mystery doctor seemed to be the key. 'Who is this doctor?' he asked.

'Affirmative,' responded K9 logically and automatically.

Sarah Jane looked at Brendan, taking him in as if he'd just

arrived from outer space, so remote had he become from the present. How often had that question been asked! How was she going to explain to a rather literal-minded fourteen-year-old the existence of a Time Lord from Gallifrey who moved in mysterious ways in space and time in apparent defiance of conventional physics. Brendan might be able to accept the fact of a mechanical dog since it was, after all, a sort of extension of Meccano or Leggo (she hoped K9 couldn't thought read as well as talk). But seeing was believing. How would she begin to describe the Doctor's TARDIS without it being on view? She decided to duck the issue completely.

She looked Brendan squarely in the eye. 'The Doctor,' she announced coolly, 'is a very great friend of mine.' She turned happily back to the Doctor's amusing gift. 'How is he, K9?' As she heard herself voice the question it suddenly sounded impertinent in view of the gift's august origins. She made amends hastily. 'I may call you K9?'

'It is my designation, Mistress.'

Such was the imprint of the mechanical dog's personality on Sarah Jane that she went bubbling on, having mentally anthropomorphised him. 'How is he?' Instantly she remembered her metal companion had been shut up in an attic in Croydon for . . . how many years was it . . . three?

'No available data,' announced K9 crisply.

'Yes, silly of me,' said Sarah Jane, her cheeks beginning to tingle in shame. 'You haven't been around, have you?'

'What is the Earth year?' asked K9.

'1981. December the eighteenth,' said Sarah Jane.

'In my memory,' went on K9 without hesitation, 'the Doctor last spoke in one-nine-seven-eight Earth years. He said, "Give Sarah Jane Smith my fondest love. Tell her I shall remember her always." '

Much moved Sarah Jane turned her face away as she stifled a small sob. *Give Sarah Jane Smith my fondest love.* 'Thank you, K9,' she sniffed softly.

Brendan had been listening to and looking at this exchange with a mounting excitement that he could contain no longer. 'You're a computer!' he burst out.

'Affirmative.'

'And a robot?'

'Affirmative.'

To demonstrate the confirmation K9 glided smoothly away over the carpet and then, coming to a stop, turned to face his new owner. Brendan went wild.

'I say! Just look at that! He's fantastic!'

'Negative,' corrected K9. 'An efficient machine.'

Brendan turned to Sarah Jane suddenly bereft of words. This was unbelievable. Who, for instance, would believe it at school? Here was a thinking, talking, free-moving, even debating mechanism. He turned to look in wonder at K9. 'What a find,' he murmured.

'A find,' repeated Sarah Jane with a face dominated by finely arched eyebrows.

'Well, yes,' said Brendan lamely.

'He's not a find. He's a present.'

'That's what I mean,' fibbed Brendan, who was then inspired. 'A Christmas present. A fabulous Christmas present.'

'*My* Christmas present!'

'Oh, all right then,' said a dashed Brendan. It was dreadfully unfair. What could Sarah possibly know about computers? 'But you'll let me play with him sometimes, won't you?'

K9 blinked. That is to say, he re-routed the circuit that would have given him voice. It wasn't that his feelings were hurt, since he had none to hurt, but he was programmed to detect and correct inaccuracies of communication and he repudiated the verb 'to play' as a fitting activity for a sophisticated assembly such as himself. It would be an abuse of high technology, an affront to the variegated skills that had brought him into being. They'd be putting him on a lead next. Then the one recognisable as a young boy redeemed himself as he turned and asked, 'Tristate bus driver?'

'Affirmative,' crooned K9.

'Bus driver?' echoed a mystified Sarah Jane anticipating the appearance from nowhere of a uniformed member of a public transport system. Brendan seized the opportunity for a subtle revenge. 'A bus in this sense,' he said in a lordly fashion, 'isn't something you buy a ticket to sit in. It's a microchip distributing data throughout a mother-board.'

'Oh,' said Sarah Jane. Brendan, turning to K9, pressed home his advantage.

'And UART?'

'Affirmative,' droned K9.

Sarah Jane knew what she was getting into. She was, after all, an investigative journalist and had had her fair share of know-alls who knew all there was to know about driving tractors, shooting clay pigeons, and computers. She said, 'What's UART?'

Brendan and K9 answered in unison, 'Universal Asynchronous Receiver Transmitter.'

'I see,' said Sarah Jane perceiving only that she was bested and deciding that nature and the know-all should take their inevitable course. But Brendan had already forgotten about Sarah Jane so intent was he on K9. 'Nuclear battery?' he asked.

'Affirmative.'

'Self-charging?'

'Affirmative.'

Brendan was so excited he performed a little jig. 'And I'll bet you have a laser scan bubble memory.'

'Affirmative.'

'I just knew it!'

Sarah Jane closed her eyes resignedly. This was far worse than she thought. She suffered the overwhelming conviction that two mammoth machine-made intellects were ganging up on her. She hadn't a chance. Not only was she ignorant of this outlandish mumbo-jumbo, she had no wish to banish that ignorance. When that state was blissful 'twas folly to be wise. She became aware that Brendan was talking to her rapidly with fanatically shining eyes. 'There's this hunk of crystal with little magnetic bubbles in it. They're so microscopic they need a laser beam to scan them. It means he's got an integrated memory like the human brain.'

'Better,' said K9.

'Well, quicker,' admitted Brendan.

'Quicker and better.'

Worse and worse, thought Sarah Jane. And then it

occurred to her that here might be the means to resolve the mystery surrounding Aunt Lavinia. If the Doctor had anything to do with the genesis of K9 or if in K9's memory there was awareness of the Doctor's methodology then K9 could be a mechanism complex and sophisticated enough to comprehend intuition and, what was more, female intuition. She interrupted the bickering. 'Oh, please don't start arguing. It'll all be above my head anyway.' She turned to the Doctor's gift. 'K9, perhaps you can help.'

'Mistress,' agreed K9.

'My aunt left here suddenly a couple of weeks ago and she's not been in touch. And it's not like her. And I've got this feeling . . . this intuition . . . that there's something wrong. Now, what would the Doctor . . . what would you do?'

K9's reply was instant and disappointing, 'Insufficient data, Mistress.'

'Oh, well,' sighed Sarah Jane. 'I just thought I'd ask.'

'But K9 hadn't finished. 'Curiosity,' he droned, 'cause of annihilation of feline species but also only means to human knowledge.'

The re-phrasing of the popular adage delighted Brendan, particularly since the proposition expressed was free of the traditional bias expected in the canine species. There could be nothing more objective than a computer. 'Hey, that's good!' enthused Brendan. He turned to Sarah Jane. 'Isn't that good?' But she, in her disappointment, took a quite different view.

She looked K9 straight in his lighted eyes and defied him to read her uncomplimentary thought at his profound announcement. Pompous pup! Out loud she said: 'That does it!'

'What?' enquired Brendan.

'I'm going out.'

'Where?'

'I don't know. I'll indulge my curiosity,' she said with edge. 'I imagine you two will be able to amuse yourselves.'

Brendan was as oblivious of Sarah Jane's heavy irony as was K9. 'You bet,' he said happily.

'Affirmative,' agreed K9.

5

The Black Art

Sarah Jane closed the front door grumpily. Daylight had gone and there was little other light to see by. What there was came from the distant lamp-post in the road near the Manor gates. She'd decided to call at the Post Office and talk to the Gregson woman but she wouldn't take the car. She'd had enough driving for one day. The MGB was where she'd left it and she gave it an affectionate pat as she made off down the drive. She'd put it away when she got back.

Her heart came into her mouth as she heard movement on the gravel behind her. Then, just as suddenly, she guessed who it might be. She was right.

'Not using the car, Miss?'

Sarah Jane turned to face the barely visible shape by the MGB. Where had the man come from? That was the frightening question. As it was earlier that afternoon, so it was this time. Gravel. Gravel from the front door to the car and for a like distance in every direction. How had the man got there? All she'd heard was the single crunch as if the man had landed from the air. Sarah Jane put the thought from her as nonsense but she had to keep a conscious grip on herself for she was still frightened. 'No,' she said. 'Mr Tracey, is it?'

'Yes, Miss. Best not leave it here if you're not going to use it.'

'I was going to put it away later.'

'I'll do it for you if you'll give me the key.'

Sarah Jane felt directly threatened. This wasn't an offer of help so much as a demand. She said, 'Thank you, but that's all right. I'll do it myself now.'

'Bit of a bother, Miss,' said the dark shape. 'It means moving a tractor and my car and the Commander's. Better if I do it. Less bother, and it is dark.'

Sarah Jane hesitated. So that was it. The message was clear. She was displacing Tracey or the Commander or both. She was in the way – an intruder. But no more so than Aunt Lavinia had been.

If she was to stay here she'd have to come to terms with this situation. She was on the point of apologising for being a nuisance when she thought better of it. She'd go along with the man, signal her trust. She sensed it would be unwise to alienate him further.

'That's very kind of you,' she said and felt in her bag for her car keys. Tracey's feet disturbed the gravel noisily as he shortened the distance between them, reawakening her mystification and her dread. She held out the keys fearfully, thankful in one way for the dark that cloaked her fear. She shuddered as his fingers brushed hers. 'Just pop them through the letterbox,' she said as lightly as she could. Tracey said nothing and she bade him a good night, as she turned away, half in the hope that it would be the last she'd see of him for one day. As she walked unsteadily down the drive she was thankful to hear the MGB started and driven away with care.

The village of Hazelbury Abbas was nothing if not compact: the church, a pub and the general store and sub Post Office which Sarah Jane reached in four minutes without hurrying. She'd met nobody on the way and no more than two cars had passed her at a sedate pace, both driven by elderly women. Or were they? She smiled to herself as she remembered her display of bad temper on the road that afternoon. Lights remained on in the shop but a reversible card on the far side of the glass door had been turned to provide the information that the establishment was closed. Sarah Jane glanced at her watch. It was barely five-twenty. Clearly the tempo in deepest Dorset was downbeat.

She looked about for a bell push, found none, and then peered through the door. The glass was impeccably clean as was the small shop beyond it. A tiny counter faced the simple window display and another counter ran at a right angle towards the diminutive Post Office counter and grille. A flap in the larger counter gave access to the other shelves in the shop and was set in front of a door that obviously led to the rest of the premises.

At a few seconds after twenty past five Sarah Jane felt justified in tapping on the door. She tapped a second time and was about to turn away irritably when the door behind the counter opened and a woman appeared making gestures that indicated politely that the notice on the door be read. Sarah Jane made the counter move of looking pointedly at her watch.

The woman, with a small show of impatience, came through the flap in the counter on her way to the door. She was of medium height but stockily built and wore a neat flowered cotton dress protected by a clean white apron. About fifty-five, Sarah Jane thought, with well-cared for greying hair above a broad face with wide apart eyes and a generous mouth. The woman unlocked the door and opened it a little way.

'I'm closed, m'dear.'

'But it's not yet half past five.'

'I close early Fridays.'

'Sorry. I'm new here. Mrs Gregson, is it?'

'That's right.' A sudden thought came to Lily Gregson causing an abrupt change of mien and expression. 'You wouldn't be from the Manor? Doctor Smith's niece?'

'Yes, I am.'

'That's different,' said Lily Gregson warmly. 'Come in! Come in!' And she swept wide the door in the manner of the genie showing Aladdin the cave.

'Thank you.' Sarah Jane accepted the invitation with relief that time wasn't to be wasted. Lily Gregson closed and locked the shop door and led the way through the counter and the door beyond. Sarah Jane found herself in a small, cosy living-room, comfortably furnished and as neat as a pin. A coal fire glowed and a kettle still steamed on a trivet. Set on a low table in front of the sofa was a gleaming white cloth upon which lay a teapot, cup and saucer, milk jug and sugar bowl. There was also a slice of fruit cake on a small plate.

'I've just made myself a cup of tea. Would you like one?'

51

'Very much indeed,' accepted Sarah Jane gratefully, remembering the neglected teapot at the Manor.

'Sit you down,' said Lily Gregson. 'Make yourself at home.'

'Thank you.'

As Sarah Jane made herself comfortable in an easy chair the older woman toddled off into her small kitchen. Her hostess came back carrying another cup and saucer and another piece of cake. The unexpected reminder of the Doctor notwithstanding Sarah Jane hadn't felt so happy all day.

'I always make myself a cup when I close,' Lily was saying. 'Then I put my feet up for five minutes before I clear up and do the paperwork. It's the only way I can keep up with that blessed VAT. Should never have been allowed, that. Never!'

'What about Mr Gregson?' asked Sarah Jane politely.

'Passed on, poor soul,' said Lily with no noticeable sentiment. 'All too much for him.'

'The shop?' asked Sarah Jane, wondering what massive turnover Hazelbury Abbas could muster that would overwork a man and wife.

'Oh, not the shop,' said Lily with a merrily wicked laugh, 'More me, I shouldn't wonder. Milk and sugar?'

'Milk and no sugar, thanks.'

Sarah Jane smiled in slightly shocked amusement and found herself watching the woman's hands which were broad and capable and deft as they sped over the tea-table. They were the hands of a strong and energetic woman. Poor Mr Gregson. Perhaps she *had* been too much for him. Sarah Jane couldn't help feeling that the energy rather contradicted the lifestyle reflected from the fact that she'd been made more than welcome without any enquiry about the reason for her visit.

Lily Gregson handed Sarah Jane her tea and then offered her the piece of cake. 'You've got to try a piece of this. I made it myself.'

'Thank you,' said Sarah Jane, remembering she was peckish, 'it looks lovely.'

The relaxed grocer and sub post mistress sipped delicately at her tea and asked, 'You're not in a hurry or anything, dear, are you?'

Sarah Jane smiled, wondering if it would make any difference to her hostess if she admitted she was. 'No,' she said, 'oh no.'

'Good,' said Lily. 'I like a bit of company.'

Sarah Jane bit into her cake which was quite delicious. She liked this woman in spite of the even tenor of her ways and was content to leave the pacing of their meeting to her. 'Lovely cake,' she mumbled.

'Thank you, dear,' said Lily. 'I knew you'd like it. Now then, what can I do for you?'

'I wanted to send a cable.'

'Ah,' said the sub post mistress, looking at her watch.

'To Reuters in New York,' went on Sarah Jane.

'No need to come here for that. You've got the telephone, haven't you?'

'There was something else, Mrs Gregson.'

Lily chuckled merrily. 'Call me Lily,' she said. 'Your Auntie always did.'

'Did she send me a telegram . . . or whatever it's called nowadays . . . before she left? Through you, I mean?'

A troubled look clouded the merriment from Lily's face. 'No, dear. She was never near me for well over a fortnight. Worried me, it did. Didn't even drop in to say goodbye. Not like her, that. Not a bit like her.'

Again Sarah Jane had come to a blank wall, a dead end. She felt wretched again, and frightened in spite of Lily Gregson's welcome and their common concern. If *she* had no news of Aunt Lavinia who on Earth would? Her line of thought switched instantly to Juno Baker, who had introduced herself as a friend of Aunt Lavinia. It could be her last hope. As her mind fixed on the Lodge opposite the church, she was only partly conscious of Lily saying something. 'I beg your pardon?' she said.

'I said was she absent-minded, your Auntie?'

'I don't think so,' said Sarah Jane. 'Not really, no more than most of us.'

Lily Gregson sipped her tea thoughtfully. 'A lot of clever people are, I've found. Say they're going to do something and then forget about it completely.' She put down her cup and prodded with a deft forefinger at her temple. 'Too much going on in here.'

Sarah Jane had never heard absent-mindedness better described. 'I think you've got a point there, Lily,' she said.

'You're clever too, your Auntie tells me. Work for a newspaper, don't you?'

'Well, newspapers,' clarified Sarah Jane, 'and magazines, that sort of thing. Whatever's going, really. I'm what's called a freelance.'

'Oh, yes,' said Lily nibbling on a piece of her cake and picking up her cup. 'That must take you about a bit.'

'A bit,' admitted Sarah Jane. 'I only got back from Africa today. Ran into a spot of trouble there.'

'Lot of trouble in Africa,' remarked Lily consolingly and incuriously. 'Fancy another piece of cake?'

Sarah Jane was hungry and tempted. Lily's cake was the best she could remember. But she'd made up her mind to accept Juno Baker's invitation and wanted to be at the Lodge opposite the church as soon as possible. 'No, thank you,' she said, and added, 'but don't think I'm not tempted.'

'Ah, temptation,' said Lily enigmatically. 'Nothing to do with a good piece of cake, m'dear. On holiday now, are you?'

'Half and half,' said Sarah Jane. 'I have to do a piece for a magazine and then make a start on a book.'

'That's nice,' said Lily contentedly. She nibbled at another piece of cake. 'Your Auntie wrote for the papers. Well, to the *Echo*. Letters and that.'

'Oh? Did she?'

'Upset some people,' said Lily laconically.

Sarah Jane was immediately on the alert. It was the first intimation that Aunt Lavinia was anything but popular in the village. 'What people?' she asked.

'Oh, people,' said Lily non-committaly. And then: 'People with funny ideas.'

'What funny ideas?'

'Witchcraft,' said Lily concisely.

'Witchcraft,' echoed Sarah Jane, quite suddenly visited by an unidentifiable intuition. 'Witchcraft?'

'Wrote to the *Echo* about it, she did.'

'Aunt Lavinia?'

'That she did. Upset some people. Understandable really. They're a bit sensitive around here about that. It's traditional, you see.'

Sarah Jane didn't see, but she wanted to know more. 'Is it?'

'Your Auntie wouldn't have known that, of course. She's only been here about two years.'

Sarah Jane reflected that to the Lily Gregsons of English village life two years was but a grain in the shifting sands of time. Many a newcomer to a village grew old and died without becoming accepted by a close knit community. Doctor Lavinia Smith might be respected here but it was being clearly implied that she was not yet one with the people of Hazelbury Abbas and that she was never likely to be if she laughed at their traditions. For that's what she must have done in writing letters to the local press.

But Aunt Lavinia was an anthropologist and as such she must have engaged in considerable analysis of world-wide religious rites which must have included witchcraft. It was just possible that Aunt Lavinia hadn't mocked local associations. Perhaps she'd stirred a sleeping dog. Sarah Jane instantly thought of K9 and smiled inwardly at his view of curiosity. She decided to tread warily.

'I didn't know my aunt was interested in witchcraft.'

'No more she is. But a lot of people hereabouts still believe that the Black Art makes the crops grow.'

Sarah Jane was startled but did her best not to show it. 'The Black Art?'

'That's what your Auntie called it,' said Lily and then repeated, 'Upset a lot of people.'

Sarah Jane took a sip of tea to give herself time to think. More than a sleeping dog had been stirred here. If Lily Gregson was right – and there was no reason to suppose that she wasn't – witchcraft was still being practised here. If people had been upset it could only mean that those people still clung to the primitive belief that the invocation of the elemental forces of Air, Fire, Earth and Water would make the land fruitful, plentiful.

'Mrs Gregson, are you saying it's still going on?'

'Lily,' corrected her hostess. 'Am I saying what is going on?'

'The Black Art.'

Lily broke the sombre mood with a burst of merry laughter. 'Oh, no. Bless you, no! All that stopped years and years ago. Though, mind you, some time back there were goings on over in Somerset, up Wincanton way. And then there's the Cerne Abbas Giant,' she giggled.

'Giant?'

'Big man cut into the chalk on the side of the hill. Bronze Age, they say.' She giggled again. 'Ever so rude. They do say fertility rites went on there until only a few years back.'

'But if my aunt upset people, surely that . . .'

Lily came in quickly. 'Oh, no, no! Not in that way, dear. People don't like being told what to think . . . what to believe, that's all. You've got to remember that some families in the village have been here for generations. Some of 'em, if truth be known, from the time of the Romans.'

'As long as that?' said Sarah Jane, impressed. 'I'd love to meet a family with roots as far back as that. What a story!' She was smitten by an exciting thought. 'Yours wouldn't be one of them by any chance?'

Lily again laughed merrily. 'Oh, bless you, no dear. I'm a foreigner. My lot didn't come here until the Civil War.'

Brendan was enjoying himself immensely. In fact, he hadn't had so much fun for years. He'd been introduced to computers and programming at school but they were now run of the mill stuff compared with K9.

For one thing they didn't speak and, for another, there was the need to be familiar with a specific language before you could get to grips with them. None of all that with K9. You just spoke to him and that was that. It was like having a friend who knew absolutely everything there was to know. In fact it had occurred to Brendan very early in his relationship with his newfound friend what an invaluable aid he would be in exams. He'd gone so far as to discuss the possibility with K9 only to be brought down from cloud nine by a series of complex calculations, made by the computer dog, proving that transistorisation to the required degree would be impossible. Brendan had overlooked the need to put K9 in his pocket. And, as if that small oversight wasn't enough, he'd had to listen to an interminable lecture on the illogicality of cheating: to crib defeated the whole purpose of education et cetera, et cetera, et cetera. If K9 had one blemish it was his voice. It was very monotonous and it did go on. But then, to be fair, everything had to be taken on balance. K9 only spoke when spoken to. One had to be thankful for that.

Brendan shivered and put another log on the fire. That was another advantage K9 had over him; he didn't feel the cold in this large and draughty house. He didn't feel hungry either, for that matter. Brendan wondered how long Sarah Jane was going to be. He'd eaten nothing since breakfast apart from that awful cheese roll on the train. True, he'd finished off the biscuits in the kitchen but that was only one packet. Concern for his stomach steered his thoughts towards the broader issues of food production.

'Know anything about market gardening, K9?'

'Market: an abstraction for buying and selling. Gardening: activity encouraging plant life.'

All right, all right, thought Brendan. Sorry! Sloppy use of language. 'How about horticulture?'

Data on horticulture available,' obliged K9.

'Great!' said Brendan, moving to Lavinia's imposing desk and scrabbling about for writing materials. He found a notepad but had to search himself for a Biro. 'Shoot!' he said, settling himself at the desk expectantly.

'Such action confined to combat aggressor,' chanted K9.

Brendan blinked, chalking up another of K9's limitations. He was inclined to be literal-minded. *Minded*? Never mind. 'I mean, proceed with data pertaining to horticulture.' That would show him!

K9 positioned himself to view his interlocutor who was facing him from the desk, Biro poised. 'Graphic notation unnecessary,' he intoned. 'Data printout available.'

'Terrific!' exclaimed an overjoyed Brendan. There was

clearly more to learn about K9. 'All you know, then.'

The robot-computer met the enthusiasm with neutral implacability. 'Available data considerable. Suggest specifics.'

Oh, all right then, thought Brendan, registering another K9 fault: why did he always have to be right? He said: 'All right. Soil analysis.'

'For what soil sample required?'

Brendan snorted. Why hadn't he thought of that? If he wasn't careful, this mechanical omniscience would get on his nerves. He must stop thinking of the thing as human. No, that was silly. Not human, of course, but what? A pet. That was it. He must stop thinking about it as if it were alive and on four legs. He was conscious of K9's eyes fixed immovably on him and recalled, however, that he was in the presence of high intelligence. And who knows, feelings? No, that was silly too. But opinions. He might have opinions and Brendan hated to think that this super-brain might register a low opinion of his own mental processes. A little overawed, he had to admit to himself that he wanted the machine's respect. It couldn't do any harm to give credit where credit was due. 'Soil sample,' he said. 'Of course. You *are* clever, K9.'

'Affirmative,' came the prompt response.

Brendan decided to let that one go. He moved to a window and eased back a curtain. It was quite dark outside but he hadn't far to go and he remembered where he'd seen a torch. He sped from the room calling, 'Be back in a moment' and meant to add, 'Don't go away!' but it came out atavistically as, 'Stay!'

K9 defied the order by gliding nearer the fire. He'd discovered his joints were a little stiff after three years of inactivity; his oil was thick. Not having been shut down, his circuits were still active and he sifted his input for correlation and correct storage. The boy of small years was, of course, unformed and understandably ignorant. More years and proper guidance might work wonders but, 'Stay'? He'd be patting him on the head and saying, 'Good boy, K9'! next.

Brendan took the torch from a drawer in the kitchen and looked around for something else. He found what he wanted in a packet of paper napkins. He shoved a napkin into a trouser pocket and went out to the hall where he struggled into his anorak. At the front door he switched on the torch to test its capability and then went out into the darkness.

His memory of the layout of the market garden was good but he wasn't all that sure of the horticultural divisions since his visits from school hadn't been frequent. He knew about what was called The Shop and the large car park for the use of customers but the arable land extended for many acres and then there were the orchards: apples, pears and plums. He fancied it didn't much matter what earth sample he collected since it was for general analysis but it was only commonsense to suppose that an area already under cultivation might be best.

He'd not taken a great deal of notice on arrival about the disposition of crops as his mind had been on other things but he picked his way carefully in the direction of what he thought could be winter cabbage or potatoes. He passed by a couple of greenhouses and was skirting another when he heard a noise away to his right; the sound of a door closing and a number of clicking footfalls that came to an abrupt halt. Brendan turned the torch in the direction of the noise and the fudged circle of light found an old brick wall covered with rioting creeper.

The beam of the torch wandered to right and to left along the wall of the orangery until Brendan was satisfied there was nothing of interest to be seen and then it swept away between the greenhouses as Brendan went on with his quest like an outsize will-o'-the-wisp.

From his hiding place in the shrubbery at the corner of the orangery George Tracey, descendant of Publius Trescus of the Tenth Legion, watched the latest invader violate his land.

6

A Warning

Sarah Jane stood in the hall by the open front door wondering what was wrong and not a little aware that she might be imagining things. When she had let herself into the Manor she'd not expected to be greeted but she had expected noise of some sort or the other. Brendan was, after all, a very noisy person.

She glanced at her watch, discovering the time to be half past six. She's been with Lily Gregson a long time. Half past six and not a sound from the television set. That, for a start, wasn't consistent with what she knew of Brendan's insatiable viewing.

She put that infernal bunch of keys back into her bag, closed the front door gently and quietly approached the sitting-room, half-expecting to be met by something calamitous. What she saw did, in one way, give her cause for concern. The television set in the far corner presented a grey, blank face neglected by Brendan who was squatting on the floor by K9 and so absorbed by the contents of an immensely long screed that he didn't even look up as she came into the room.

'Well,' exhaled Sarah Jane, 'wonders will never cease. I expected to be blasted out of house and home by *Top of the Pops* or something.'

'Not on tonight,' said Brendan matter-of-factly. He held up the print-out. 'Look, Sarah, K9's done a complete soil analysis and, what's more, comprehensive chemical treatment for healthy advanced yield.'

'Well, well,' said Sarah Jane. 'Nothing about witchcraft?'

'How d'you mean?' Brendan didn't get the connection and was disappointed that Sarah hadn't been more enthusiastic about this news.

'Never mind.' She stirred some neglected soil with the toe of her shoe. 'You're getting a bit old to be nagged about wiping your feet when you come in. Look at that!'

'Oh, sorry,' said and uncontrite Brendan, brushing the earth back onto the shredded paper napkin, 'that's what we were using for the analysis. Did you find anything out about Aunt Lavinia?'

'Nothing that helps,' said Sarah Jane. 'I came back to tell you I'm going to accept that invitation.'

'What invitation?'

'From our neighbours, the Bakers. I'm going over there for a drink.'

Brendan thought for the merest fraction of a second. 'What about us?' he said, before he was forced to remind himself that K9 had no complaining stomach. 'What about me?'

'What about you?'

'What about something to eat? I'm starving.'

Here we go, thought Sarah Jane: chief cook and bottle washer to Brendan Richards for the duration of the Christmas holidays! 'We'll have something when I get back,' she said, remembering the contents of the refrigerator. 'Peel some potatoes!'

'*What?*' said a startled Brendan.

'I said, peel some potatoes.'

'Oh . . .' said Brendan.

'Yes,' said Sarah Jane and was gone.

Brendan looked dejectedly at the print-out, his euphoria dissipated by the chill wind of kitchen chores. 'Help, K9,' he said.

'In what context?' asked K9.

'Potatoes,' said Brendan glumly.

'A tuber brought to United Kingdom from New World by Sir Walter Raleigh. Edible by *homo sapiens* when subjected to heat.'

'I know all that, you idiot!' said an exasperated Brendan. 'But can you peel them?'

'Negative,' droned K9.

*

Sarah Jane had decided to walk to the Bakers. It was absurd to think of driving such a short distance even if she knew where to look for the MGB. She'd leave the problem of the complicated parking until the morning. Leaving behind the Manor gates and the solitary street lamp, the way became dark. In conservation areas such as this street lighting was resisted at all levels since it inevitably meant the introduction of stark concrete posts and fluorescent lamps; the cheap cost-effective standardization not to be tolerated in a village of outstanding beauty by its inhabitants or, for that matter, by the tourists who flocked to it from all over the world.

Once past the Old Mill there was light from the pub and the going was easy down North Street with the light that leaked into the road from the twin lines of thatched cottages. Sarah Jane reflected that generations of villagers had passed this way at night without fear of molestation but, even so, she found herself glancing occasionally at the innocent sounds of closing doors or windows and muffled domestic chatter.

Beyond the school house Lily Gregson's store was now dark but soon the outline of the church became visible in the light from the house opposite in the driveway of which a number of cars were parked. The Lodge was a large Jacobean house partly masked from the road by a fringe of beech trees. Sarah Jane had never given it a lot of attention before: the beauty of the church dominated the scene.

As she tacked her way through the parked cars she saw confirmation of her misgivings in the rooms beyond undrawn curtains. Men and women stood about in small groups holding glasses and smiling at one another. She'd come to talk to Juno Baker. It was to be hoped that her role as hostess wouldn't interfere with this and it was to be hoped that as a guest she wouldn't be trapped in a corner and find it necessary to be forced into self-introduction elsewhere. She rang the doorbell.

The door was immediately opened by a Juno Baker arrayed in a black and silver dress as distinctive as the figure it has been designed to adorn. 'You'll be Sarah Jane Smith,' she said.

'Yes.'

'Juno Baker. I'm so glad you could make it. Come in!'

Sarah Jane entered the warm comfort of the expansive hall feeling underdressed and dowdy. Such was her concern for Aunt Lavinia that she'd not thought about a change of clothes and remained in those in which she'd travelled all day.

'Let me take your coat,' cooed Juno, adding, as Sarah Jane fumbled with her capacious shoulder bag, 'And you'd better let me have that too.' A moment's hesitation before: 'Unless you'll want to powder your nose.'

Sarah Jane hated her. She looked at the mocking eyes and the smile on the sensuous lips and was glad she'd come in her travelling tatts. If her nose was shiny it would jolly well remain shiny, so there! 'Thanks,' she said briskly surrendering the bag with unnecessary force and shrugging out of her leather jacket.

Juno moved with infinite grace to a long line of hooks set in the panelled wall at the foot of the staircase in the well of which stood a giant Christmas tree beautifully decked and glowing with the light of candles. A tape was playing carols sung by a Cambridge college choir at a discreet level under the chatter of guests punctuated by laughter. Juno was back at her side. 'Come and meet Howard,' she said and led the way into a generous sitting-room through knots of conventionally dressed carousers who watched covertly the passage of the strange and shabby young girl to the enormous silver punch bowl at which Howard Baker presided.

'Howard. Sarah Jane Smith,' introduced Juno with what sounded to Sarah Jane like a note of triumph. Howard beamed handsomely and pudgily upon the new arrival and ladled a colourful liquid into a glass.

'Welcome to Hazelbury Abbas,' he said. 'Delighted you could come.' He handed her the glass. 'Fruit cup. Not so innocuous as it looks. It'll cheer you up.' And, so saying, he moved off, bearing an elegant crystal and silver flagon on a replenishing mission.

'He's right,' said Juno. 'Come and meet people.'

Sarah Jane was determined to get what she came for. 'I'm sorry, Mrs Baker, but . . .'

'Juno,' corrected her hostess.

'Yes, thank you. It's just that I'm very worried about my aunt.'

'Why, dear? Is something wrong?'

'I can't help thinking there is. It's very unlike her to go off as she has without a word. And it's a fortnight now and still no word. I don't even know where she is. I thought you might know.'

'I saw her to say goodbye the day she left. She was perfectly all right then. But she didn't tell me exactly where she was going. There was no reason why she should. And I think you're worrying needlessly.' Juno extended a beautifully manicured hand and squeezed Sarah Jane's arm reassuringly. 'Give her time, my dear. Lavinia's an obsessive. She'll remember to get in touch with you when she's cleared her mental decks and not before. I know her of old.'

Sarah Jane's positive dislike of the woman led her to doubt a long friendship with her aunt, if there were friendship at all. From what she knew of Aunt Lavinia, and what she could see of this woman, they had very little, if anything, in common. 'How long *have* you known my aunt?'

Juno Baker studied the suspicion on Sarah Jane's pert face with tolerant amusement. 'How long? Since she moved here. Two years, isn't it? We natives are usually reserved with foreigners but we took to her at once. But I'll not deny it was because she was something of a celebrity.'

Sarah Jane, still very much on edge, was startled by the tense used. '*Was*?'

Juno's party face took on a strained expression. She looked past Sarah Jane as if seeking something or someone. 'Still is, of course.' Her eyes resettled on Sarah Jane's untouched glass. 'Take a good swig at that! It'll make you less prickly.'

Sarah Jane was suddenly ashamed of her churlishness. Even if she disliked the woman good manners demanded that she made no display of it. 'I'm sorry,' she said. 'It's just that I can't help feeling . . .' She left the expression of her feelings in the air.

'Of course you can't,' declared Juno. 'What you need is distraction. You're a journalist. There's someone here you simply *must* meet.'

She led Sarah Jane through numbers of her gossiping guests who, in the main, talked animatedly to their companions with their eyes firmly fixed elsewhere, to a small alcove off the sitting-room where an overweight man of fifty was staring intently at something on the wall. As the women entered the alcove he turned to face them and Sarah Jane took professional note of the thinning hair, the small, haunted blue eyes and the broken capillaries on the nose and cheeks that spoke of an over-indulgence in alcohol. There was no way for her to know that she was face to face with a witch, a member of the coven that had celebrated the esbat at the last full moon.

Henry Tobias smiled genially at his hostess. 'Juno, my dear, I've not seen this before, have I?' He pointed to a long, black-handled knife that adorned the wall.

'No, I don't think you can have,' said Juno with a quick look at Sarah Jane. 'It was given to me by a friend.'

'Fascinating,' said Tobias. 'You know what it is, I suppose?'

'I was told it's an athame,' said Juno coolly.

'What's an athame?' asked Sarah Jane.

'It's a witch's ceremonial knife,' said Tobias with a wide fruit-cup smile.

'Henry Tobias, Sarah Jane Smith,' said Juno by way of a belated introduction. 'Henry's the editor of the *Echo*.'

Brendan dried his hands on a kitchen towel and looked at the saucepan full of peeled potatoes with a certain satisfaction. No one could say he didn't show willing. He was watched by K9 who had taken up a position on the stone flags between the kitchen table and the gas cooker. Brendan had lessened the tedium of his task by probing K9's potential with a rapid bombardment of questions all brilliantly fielded by the robot-computer. They had just come to the end of an exchange stimulated by K9's observation that the size of the potato peelings dwarfed that of the peeled potatoes and that this was undesirable because the germinal layer of the tuber lay immediately below the skin. K9 had gone on to drone that the discarded peelings were of greater dietary value than the tiny, naked knobs sitting in the saucepan. This, in turn, had inspired Brendan to a discursive summary of the diverse ways of cooking the spud in order to draw attention from his hurried potato peeling technique.

'That in metal container remains unfit to eat,' persisted K9.

'*You're* not being asked to eat them,' said Brendan tartly.

'Ontogenesis retarded,' retorted K9.

'What on Earth does that mean?'

'In infantile terms: "you won't grow up to be a big boy." '

Oh, you go to . . . thought Brendan. During the last uncomfortable ten minutes he'd come to the conclusion that inheriting this miniature mechanical monster wasn't as exciting as he'd first thought. He rubbished about in his mind for some topic he might introduce that could save his face. It would have to be something technical to give him any sort of parity with the know-all hound.

'Well, that's that in here,' he said. 'Let's get back to the sitting-room.' He turned from the sink to see K9 already disappearing through the open kitchen door and followed, switching off the light. He crossed the hall to see K9 waiting patiently by the closed sitting-room door. He grinned joyfully and savoured his satisfaction as he switched off the main light leaving a lamp on a side table to greet Sarah's return. Here was something, at least, where he had the edge: the robot couldn't open doors! Brendan couldn't resist rubbing it in. 'Sorry, K9, I forgot you can't open doors.'

'Means of access to chamber available but method destructive,' said K9 equably.

Brendan's grin grew wider. He knew a bluff when he heard one. He opened the door and allowed K9 to precede him. He was in the act of tossing a log on the fire when he remembered something from the computer lab at school which might restore his esteem *vis-à-vis* K9.

'You have five logic gates, haven't you, K9?'

'Affirmative.'

'And you can rely on the logic gates and your memory? You don't need updating from time to time with a "piggyback board"?'

There was the slightest hesitation before K9's reply; long enough to give Brendan hope that he might have got him at last.

'Affirmative, affirmative,' said K9.

Better and better, thought Brendan. He'd got him repeating himself. Or could it be mechanical failure? 'Affirmative, affirmative?' he mocked.

'To both questions; affirmative,' said K9 affably.

Brendan was jiggered if he was going to be outdone. 'But you hesitated, didn't you, K9?'

'Required to scan inverted negative in second question,' explained K9. 'Syntactically undesirable,' he added evenly.

For a fraction of a second Brendan carefully considered kicking the little beast to the other side of the room but intelligence prevailed. For one thing the little so-and-so could be damaged and his feelings would hardly be hurt and, for another thing, K9 was compounded of solid stuff. A little more solid than Brendan's foot. He turned away fuming and stared sightlessly at a row of Aunt Lavinia's books.

In the depths of the hall darkened by the brooding staircase the back door opened noiselessly and two figures stood silhouetted against the risen moon. George Tracey slipped into the hall followed reluctantly by his son Peter. The older man pulled the boy in front of him impatiently and hissed, 'Come on! What's the matter with you?'

'I don't like this,' muttered the terrified Peter.

'I'm not *asking* you to do it, I'm *telling* you to!' breathed his father. 'She's out, I tell you, and he's in there where the light's are on. Now, come on!'

Peter shied away from his father's shove and knocked into a side table bringing down a brass bowl of dried flowers and the lamp, plunging the hall into darkness. Peter gasped and ran for the back door only to be grabbed by Tracey and pulled violently away from it.

In the sitting-room Brendan and K9 were both facing the door. 'Sarah?' called Brendan. It wasn't like her to crash about like that. He hurried out to the hall to be faced, in the poor light filtering from behind him, with the frightening spectacle of two dark figures struggling with each other.

Brendan was so shocked he wanted to run but he held his ground. The taller of the two figures pushed the other aside and advanced on Brendan who reached for the light switch, but Tracey was before him grasping Brendan's arm and trying to force it behind the boy's back. Brendan cried, 'Get off!' and lashed out with his other arm, knocking Tracey off balance.

Peter stood back, uncertain what to do, watching his father battling against Brendan's flailing arms. In a torment of doubt Peter forced himself to his father's aid and managed to secure one of Brendan's arms. Brendan's fear had been replaced by anger. He growled, grunted and fought with all his strength. As he contended valiantly against unequal odds he little knew that help was very close at hand.

K9 came through from the sitting-room fast and positioned himself to face the mêlée. A tube-like protrusion jutted suddenly from his front elevation just as a violent swing from Brendan flung Peter towards K9. A blinding beam of light burst from the tube and impinged on the unfortunate Peter who cried out in shock and collapsed on the floor.

Both Brendan and Tracey had been facing K9 when he used his blaster and they reacted to the phenomenon in different ways. Brendan was gaping in astonished admiration and Tracey was goggle-eyed with terror for his immortal soul. As K9 advanced towards the fallen Peter, Tracey screamed and backed away. He stumbled, fell and, still screaming, scrambled on all fours to the back door where he regained his feet and fled into the night.

If Brendan had been frightened before he was now terrified at the noise made by Tracey. He'd never heard a man scream before and it was unnerving. He switched on the main hall light and watched K9 probe closely at Peter Tracey's face.

'I say, K9, thanks. What was it you did?' he managed to get out at last.

'Infra-sound directional beam at low level induces temporary paralysis,' explained K9, completely above Brendan's

head. 'Aggressor rendered insensible. Suggest he is pinioned.'
And without more ado he glided off to the back door in
pursuit of the terror-stricken Tracey.

Left alone Brendan felt the onset of panic. He looked down
at the youth on the floor in total bewilderment. He was little
older than himself. Who was he, and who was the other man,
and why were they here, and why did they attack him? And,
perhaps most important of all, how had they got in? Sarah
had made sure all windows and doors were locked. He began
to shiver. Then he remembered K9's suggestion about the
'insensible aggressor' and looked about him for something to
tie the attacker up.

Peter Tracey groaned and moved his head and Brendan
realised with horror that without K9 he was completely
helpless. As the youth on the floor moved again Brendan
edged this way and that trying to think of how to tie . . . *that's
it*! That was it! Brendan tore off his tie and knelt quickly to
secure the intruder's hands behind his back.

Now he felt better, less dependent on K9. He was already
rehearsing the story he would tell them at school. He pulled
the knot tight and then hurried to the back door to check on
K9. Everything under the moon seemed still and, from what
he'd just seen, K9 could look after himself very well.

He left the door open and hurried back to his prisoner who
was groaning and trying to get up. Brendan had regained his
confidence and the youth was helpless and looked frightened.
There could be no harm in giving him a hand up. Once on his
feet Peter Tracey shrugged off Brendan's helping hand and
lurched towards the back door. 'Hang about!' said Brendan,
catching his prisoner by an arm.

'Let me go!' pleaded Peter.

'What about answers to a couple of questions?' responded
Brendan.

'Please!'

'Who are you?'

The fear in Peter's eyes gave way to tears and he began to
blubber, making Brendan feel very superior indeed. 'Come
on now, pull yourself together!' he said. 'Nobody's going to
hurt you.'

Peter recovered sufficiently to blurt out, 'You've got to leave here. You and the girl. You've got to get away!' Brendan's recently found confidence began to ebb. There was no mistaking his prisoner's sincerity.

'Why? And why did you go for me like that?'

'Please let me go!' begged Peter.

'And who was that other man?'

Terrified by the question Peter tugged hard to free himself.

'Oh, no you don't,' said Brendan. 'You're going to stay here until I've talked to Sarah. Miss Smith,' he added, not wanting to admit his attacker to the family circle.

Peter Tracey's fear was yielding to anger. 'Don't be a fool!' he said vehemently. 'Get away before they get you! Before they get you both!'

'Who's they?' demanded a fascinated Brendan, growing in stature by the second.

'Get away!' shouted Peter hysterically. 'Just get away! Go on! Now! *Before it's too late!*'

7

K9 Blunders

George Tracey wanted to run for his life, less in fear of death than in fear of damnation but he dared not break cover lest he draw the hell-hound to him. From his hiding place in the packing shed he watched, with a dry mouth and a pounding heart, the white dog as it prowled for him in the lanes between the greenhouses. Every time the hound from Hell changed direction Tracey moaned a quiet prayer to Hecate, begging forgiveness for his failure to take the boy. There, in the hall of the Manor, Hecate had sent her avenging familiar to strike down his only son, consigning him to eternal damnation. Even as he prayed he knew there could be no forgiveness. Those who lived within the dominion of the Infernal Regions could expect no mercy. He watched the hell-hound, gleaming in the moonlight, as it moved out of sight. Tracey considered flight but was rooted with terror.

K9 continued to turn in varied arcs in an attempt to get an infra-red reading on his quarry, but he was baffled at every turn by a multiplicity of choices. His circuits informed him of many bloodheated targets, but what they couldn't tell him was that most of his soundings were reflected from animals other than *homo sapiens*: something only to be expected in a rural area where horses, cattle, sheep and pigs abounded, to say nothing of foxes, rabbits and the nocturnal cat.

He had decided to abandon his search and return to the Manor when an owl left the trees to his left with a flurry of wings that suggested human disturbance. K9 turned instantly and glided forward to investigate. After a few yards his way was blocked by a large, metal oil tank and he turned sharply to come face to face with a man smaller than himself wearing a floppy hat, a white beard and holding a fishing rod. K9 knew his speed was such that he would be unable to pull up in time to avoid the sudden death or injury of this surprisingly tiny human beings, so veered sharply away without knowing where he was going. He collided alarmingly with a fencing post that supported a stack of other posts. The stack tumbled in violent disorder and crashed into the side of a greenhouse with the brittle, protesting clanging of shattering glass. The sudden sound acted as a trigger to the terror-stricken Tracey who with a dry, coughing cry bounded from his hiding place.

In the hall Brendan and Peter Tracey had both heard the unmistakable sound of bursting glass. Brendan's thoughts were immediately with K9 and he rushed into the sitting-room, picked up the torch he'd found in the kitchen, and tore past his prisoner on the way to the back door.

'Untie me, please!' called Peter Tracey but Brendan's order of priorities listed K9 first. Peter began a desperate struggle with the tie that bound his wrists.

Brendan looked about him in the moonlight pondering which direction to take. He determined to risk exposing himself to his retreated enemy and called, 'K9!' but not too loudly. There came an answering *bleep-bleep* that could only have emanated from the robot. Brendan switched on the torch and hurried in the direction of the sound.

He was soon within sight of the greenhouses and at once associated them with the breaking glass. The double *bleep* sounded again, nearer this time, and Brendan swept his field of vision with the torch beam. The light wasn't long in finding the gaping, jagged wound, the impact of the posts having reverberated along almost all the side of the greenhouse. Brendan saw the collapsed posts at the same time as hearing another discreet double *bleep*. He sped forward, shining the torch beam on an untidy arrangement of posts leaning heavily against a large oil tank. Tell-tale reflections from K9's glossy outer surface peeped between the fallen posts.

'Are you all right, K9?' asked Brendan anxiously.

'Affirmative,' replied the trapped robot flatly, 'but in need of manumission.'

72

'Manu-what?' queried a bewildered Brendan.

A gentle whirring sound that could have been interpreted as a sigh came from underneath the posts. 'Appear to be captive slave of diminutive artefact,' expanded K9. Brendan set about releasing K9, dismissing the incomprehensible statement as possible mechanical failure due to damage, and soon had the robot free.

'Gratitude,' announced K9.

'Are you damaged in any way?' asked Brendan running anxious eyes over certain vulnerable projections that passed for ears and tail.

'Negative. Incapable self aid due to obstruction of blaster.'

'Blaster?'

K9 extended the tube-like process by way of explanation and Brendan concentrated the torch beam on it. 'That's a blaster? Is that what you used inside?' And, without waiting for an answer, went on avidly, 'What else can it do?'

'Potential adaptation considerable,' replied K9 enigmatically. He described an arc as if looking for something and then tracked to examine closely the stone manikin now lying on its side, still holding an intact fishing rod and grinning back widely.

'Request identification,' said K9.

'That,' said Brendan, 'is a garden gnome. Spelt with a "g",' he thought he'd better add.

'Garden nome spelt with a g not in my memory,' K9 appeared to moan.

'I bet it is now,' grinned Brendan.

What Sarah Jane had feared might happen had indeed happened. She was trapped with Tobias, Juno probably assuming that she would be happy talking to a fellow journalist.

She was far from happy. The man was pompous, opinionated and self-regarding and was already the worse for drink. She'd stuck with him because she could think of no better way of finding out just exactly what Aunt Lavinia had contributed to the *Echo*, hoping that it might be he who brought the subject up as she didn't want to appear too curious, too concerned about the issue. Ever since she first saw the man she'd sensed uneasy 'vibes' she couldn't explain and had made up her mind he wasn't to be trusted. In particular she'd no wish to be misquoted in the next issue of his newspaper.

But Tobias hadn't talked about her aunt. Instead he'd tried to persuade her to contribute to the paper – a weekly column on local issues, local people. Sarah Jane had had no trouble divining what that would turn out to be, and equally had absolutely no trouble at all in declining, pleading pressure of newly-commissioned work.

There finally came a point when she could bear no more of the man and she introduced Aunt Lavinia to the conversation by way of anthropology, comparing primitive cave drawings to the even more primitive modern newspaper. Tobias had been amused or, at least, he'd smiled only with his mouth while being condescendingly flattering. He was still smiling with his mouth when he said, 'You could call it a brouhaha, that's all. Your aunt wrote a letter claiming that she'd found evidence that Black Magic rites were being celebrated locally. The correspondence page was quite lively for three weeks.'

Sarah Jane was quietly angry: 'Making my aunt very unpopular.'

'Oh, I wouldn't say that,' said Tobias with his bland, mask-like smile.

'*I* would,' she countered forcefully. 'Some of these practices are outside the law.'

'You have the advantage of me,' shrugged Tobias. 'I know very little about the subject.'

'But you enjoyed printing that letter.'

'It amused me and I thought it might amuse other people. Nobody takes that sort of thing seriously any more.'

'Really?' said Sarah Jane, making it sound as if she doubted Tobias's capacity to be right about anything. A telephone had begun to ring and over Tobias's shoulder she saw Howard Baker move to answer it.

'No,' went on Tobias with something happening to his bland smile; the eyes were joining in but with lowered lids.

' 'Though I must confess I very often wonder why not. Evil *does* appear to be gaining a lot of popularity.'

Sarah Jane liked him even less. 'That's if you believe what you read in the newspapers,' she said with measured enunciation. She was delighted to see his eyelids lift like curtains to expose the watery glint behind.

'*Touché!*' said Tobias with curling lips. Sarah Jane made her point. The editor of the *North Dorset Echo* interrupted his leer long enough to slop down a little more fruit cup. That's it, thought Sarah Jane, time to go, girl. She was on the point of excusing herself when Juno Baker came up to them, her full lips stretched in a smile.

'Are you earning your drink, Henry?' asked Juno.

'Do I ever fail?' quipped the wet-lipped Tobias. 'I've been trying to persuade Miss Smith to do something for me.' Juno's eyebrows became interrogative. 'A personal column,' continued the editor.

'Gossip,' clarified Sarah Jane with deliberation. Juno's lips stretched even wider.

'How lovely!' she cooed. 'And is she going to do it?'

'No,' said Sarah Jane succinctly. 'She's not. She's taken enough on board for the moment.'

'What a pity,' murmured Juno. 'It might have livened your conservative little rag up a bit, Henry.'

'I'm very pleased for Miss Smith,' leered the vindictive Tobias. 'It's nice to be able to turn work down.'

Howard Baker approached in rather a hurry. 'Sorry to butt in,' he said, 'may I borrow my wife for a moment?' He drew Juno a little apart. 'I've got to go out.'

'Oh, Howard!'

'Excuse me,' said Sarah Jane to Tobias and moved away from him on the pretext of putting down her glass. She wanted to make her apologies and depart as quickly as possible. Brendan would be starving by this time. For a moment she was close enough to Howard Baker to hear him say: 'It won't be for long but I can't avoid it.'

'That's what you always say,' said Juno with mock annoyance. 'All right. Go on!' She began to shoo him through their guests. 'Off! Off!'

Sarah Jane was on the point of following when she felt a touch on her arm from which she recoiled as if stricken. She knew instantly who was behind the touch. She turned to find Tobias unnecessarily close with a wallet and glass in one hand and a visiting card in the other. 'Try the Cornell University Press,' he said.

'I beg your pardon?' said Sarah Jane coldly, repressing a shiver of loathing.

'If you're worried about your aunt . . . the Cornell University Press is in New York.'

'Who said I was worried?' said Sarah Jane sharply.

Tobias's breath was foetid. 'My dear, it's written all over you.' As Sarah Jane eased away he held out the card. 'If ever I can be of help, don't hesitate.'

'Thank you,' said Sarah Jane ignoring the card. 'I've already cabled Reuters in New York. Excuse me.'

As she moved after Juno the smile slipped from Tobias's face. He watched the girl go with a malevolent glint in his eyes.

The beam from Brendan's torch fluttered on and around the back door of the Manor. All appeared to be safe and the boy led the way through the open door into the hall.

'Advise caution,' intoned K9. He passed Brendan who took the advice by returning to the back door and bolting it. The prisoner was nowhere to be seen. That didn't surprise Brendan for he'd realised retrospectively that in rushing to help K9 he'd left the way clear for the frightened young man to escape.

'I tied him up, K9,' he said, by way of an apology, 'but then I heard that crash.' He passed K9 on his way to the sitting-room.

'Wait!' rapped the robot. 'I will precede.' Brendan accepted the order unreservedly. He now saw K9 with new eyes. Gone was the irritation arising from their intellectual exchanges, gone the tyranny of electronic superiority. K9 was a true friend.

'After you, K9,' he said unhesitatingly and stepped aside.

K9 glided forward into the sitting-room, stopped, described a scanning arc and announced: 'Safe to enter.'

'Thanks, K9.'

Brendan had been reasonably sure no one would be lurking in the sitting-room but, in the sinister circumstances, he was grateful the formidable K9 was taking the initiative. 'I think we'd better call the police,' he said, advancing on the telephone. Then he faltered. 'I don't know, though. I'm fourteen years old,' he sighed. 'D'you know what that means, K9?'

'Affirmative. You are fourteen Earth years old.'

Brendan sighed a second time. What could K9 know about the credibility of a fourteen-year-old in a world dominated by the hardened arteries and prejudices of the so-called adult?

'I'm what's known as a minor,' he said despondently. 'Nobody takes any notice of minors, least of all the police. And what are they going to think about you?' Brendan misinterpreted K9's silence and hurriedly sought to make amends. 'I'm sorry, K9, I didn't mean to hurt your feelings.'

'No sentient vulnerability,' explained K9. 'Rhetorical question requires no answer.' Adding, as Brendan marvelled anew, 'Suggest: contact Mistress.'

'That's it, of course, K9! Sarah will know what to do.' And Brendan pounced on the telephone directory.

There was little light in George Tracey's cottage living-room. What there was in no way reflected rural simplicity or the near poverty usually associated with those who work directly on the land. There was ample evidence of good taste and, if not opulence, of good living. What was conspicuously absent was the woman's touch, that attention to detail in the matter of inessentials that make the indefinable fabric of a home. The light came from a single candle in an ornate candlestick set on the bare top of an antique kitchen table.

Tracey looked with apprehension at the table top on which had been drawn in chalk a double circle slashed by a five-pointed star formed in a single line. He looked up from the pentacle and at the tall figure in shadow at the other side of the table; and nodded fearfully. The point of a ceremonial dagger was plunged into the centre of the pentacle: Tracey had been invited to swear a dreadful oath. He licked dry lips and cleared his throat. 'I swear by Amduscias, by Asmodeus, by Astaroth and by Arianrod that Goddess Hecate's familiar appeared to me. A dog! A shining white dog! Belching fire!'

A hand plucked the dagger from the table and Tracey fell to his knees sobbing. The dark figure remained quite still, a brooding, watching presence as the man grovelling before it struggled to speak through his tears. 'My son . . . my son . . . Peter . . . gone . . . snatched by Hell's fire. *Peter*!' He choked to a long silence and then lifted his hands pathetic-ally. 'I failed. I failed and my son has been taken from me. What must I do?'

For answer, the hand that had used the dagger pointed at the table top. Tracey scrambled to his feet, fetched a kitchen towel and wiped the table clean of chalk marks. Then he looked up again at the pervading occult presence and said quietly, 'I beg you, mighty one, what must I do?'

The long silence that followed was broken by the move-ment of the handle to the door that led directly from the exterior. Tracey whirled away from it bringing his back hard against a Welsh dresser and dislodging a plate which smashed on the floor at this feet. 'It's here,' he muttered terror-stricken. 'It's come!' He blundered about blindly screaming, 'Help me! Help me!'

The door was fumbled open by Peter Tracey whose wrists remained tied behind him. He looked at his father crouched at the foot of the stairs, his arms covering his head, and then at the figure beyond the table.

'Dad?' he said in bewilderment, 'Dad?'

Tracey uncovered his face and looked incredulously at his son. He lurched to his feet and pointed voicelessly at the still open door.

'Dad?' repeated Peter, 'are you all right?'

Tracey stumbled to the door and slammed it shut. He locked it and stood with his back pressed to it, panting for breath. His relief at seeing his son again was giving way to a slow, growing horror.

'Dad,' went on Peter, 'what happened?'

His father was unable to answer, fast held in the grip of a nameless dread.

Peter looked from one to the other and turned to show his bound wrists. 'I got knocked out and he did this to me.' He waited. 'Isn't somebody going to untie me?'

Tracey found his voice at last. 'You've led it here,' he babbled. 'Curse you! You've led it here!'

'What?' said a mystified Peter watching the terror tremble through his father out of all proportion with what had gone before. 'I've led no one. There's no one here. There was a crash outside and he ran out; so did I. Somebody's made a terrible mess of the Lane greenhouse. I hid for a bit until everything had quietened down . . . then came home.'

'The dog?' panted Tracey.

'What?'

'The dog! The dog!'

Peter hadn't ever seen K9. 'What dog?' he asked simply.

Tracey stared, wide-eyed, at his son and then turned with outstretched arms to the shadow beyond reach of the candle-light. 'I swear,' he entreated, 'I swear!'

Brendan hadn't been able to reach Sarah Jane by telephone for the reason that she was already on her way, fleeing from the execrable Tobias and a houseful of people with whom she had little in common. She stood in the sitting-room still in her leather jacket having been filled in about the eventful evening by a breathless Brendan.

'Yes, well, you're right,' she said. 'We'd better get on to the police.' On her way to the telephone she said: 'But I know I locked that back door. I know it.'

'Well, it's not been forced,' said Brendan. 'K9 took a look at it, didn't you K9?'

'Affirmative.'

'So that means they had a key,' concluded Brendan.

Sarah Jane stopped in the act of picking up the telephone. If someone else had a key that someone must be *persona grata* at the Manor. It was unlikely that the attack on Brendan was the result of the frustrated entry of a burglar. Most burglars don't have the benefit of keys. Unless, of course, they acquired the keys in some nefarious way. These attackers must be known to her, must be to do with the Manor. She had a

79

responsibility to Aunt Lavinia to do nothing hasty here. Certain questions should be asked first. She remembered Pollock's ruthless dismissal of a young member of the work force and instantly rejected all intention of reporting the incident to him. No harm, after all, had been done to Brendan. She moved away from the telephone.

'And you've no idea who this man was, the one you caught?'

'No.'

'Didn't you ask him?'

'Of course I asked him!' said an exasperated Brendan. 'What am I expected to do, torture him or something? All he kept saying was that we should get away from here.'

'But he was the one who got away by all accounts,' observed Sarah Jane with just a hint of sarcasm.

'All right, all right,' protested Brendan, 'but we had a bit of a *contretemps* with a greenhouse.'

'Bit of a *what*?'

'Somebody or something made a bit of a mess of a greenhouse,' admitted Brendan, hoping to get away with it.

'*Mea culpa*,' put in K9.

'No,' said Brendan loyally, 'it was the garden gnome.'

'Would you mind telling me what you two are talking about?'

'It doesn't matter,' muttered Brendan, deciding to let a sleeping dog lie.

'What did he look like?'

Brendan concentrated. 'About twenty or so. Gypsy looking. Lot of dark hair. And he had large eyes that stared a bit.'

Sarah Jane was rocked. Brendan had given a pretty fair description of Peter Tracey. And two men involved? Could the other one have been his father? If so, it still left the motive for the attack. Tracey had made it pretty clear that their presence was resented, but to the extent of offering physical violence? There had to be something else. She didn't like the implications. If the Traceys were faced with this it would be a case of Brendan's word against theirs. She had a sudden thought. 'Did K9 see him?'

'Description corroborated,' droned K9.

'Did K9 see him!' crowed Brendan with undisguised hero worship. 'You should have seen it!'

'Yes, his blaster,' said Sarah Jane abstractedly. 'You must demonstrate it sometime, K9.'

'Mistress,' said K9 agreeably.

'In the meantime,' continued Sarah Jane, 'we'd better lock and bolt every door and window in the place if I'm to feel safe tonight.'

'Aren't you going to get on to the police?' asked Brendan.

'Not tonight,' said Sarah Jane non-committally. 'I'll do it in the morning.'

'There is one thing,' said Brendan plaintively.

'What's that?'

'Couldn't we have something to eat first? I'm starving.'

Sarah Jane winced.

8

A Confrontation

Sarah Jane had spent a restless night. She'd fed Brendan, eating little herself, and packed him off to bed after securing firmly all doors and windows. She had then sat down with pad and pencil and sought a long session with K9. She'd put into him a whole series of random thoughts concerning the possible motive for the attack on Brendan, asking for correlation, association and analysis. The answer, arrived at in the small hours, was simple. The motive remained obscure but what was transparently clear was that the background to it was desperation, something she knew already.

What also emerged was that there must be silence about the existence of K9. A cupboard in the kitchen had been selected as a kennel, with Sarah Jane smiling at the word. The smile had become broader when K9, seeing his kennel mates to be items of domestic machinery, suggested that if discovered he should be identified as a novelty vacuum cleaner, the hose being equated to the lead by which he went 'walkies'.

Over breakfast Brendan had been suitably briefed and sworn to silence about K9. Sarah Jane had further insisted that she do the talking – *all* the talking – and that any reference to the attack on Brendan must be left to her. She then telephoned the police in West Norton. Further exchanges with K9 confirmed the logic in seeking out Peter Tracey, flushing a ferret through the hidden burrows of motive.

As she finished making up her face, Sarah Jane looked through her bedroom window and out across to the market garden. There she saw Tracey approaching the greenhouses. She tripped quickly downstairs and collected Brendan, resolving on the use of shock tactics. He and K9 were still in the kitchen engaged in learned exchanges concerning the internal combustion engine with the emphasis firmly placed on formula racing vehicles. K9 was apologetically consigned to his kennel and Sarah Jane hustled Brendan through the back door, locking it behind her.

Tracey was standing near the damaged greenhouse and had been joined by Commander Pollock and his truculent-looking dog, Jasper. As Sarah Jane and Brendan picked their way down the narrow paths that gave access to the cultivated furrows the Commander turned to greet them unsmilingly. 'Good morning. Were you disturbed by this last night?' he said, indicating the damage inflicted on the greenhouse.

'Good morning,' answered Sarah Jane carefully. 'I was out, but I think Brendan heard something, didn't you?'

'Yes,' Brendan agreed readily, 'I did hear something,' adding, with no lie, 'I *thought* it sounded like breaking glass.' He looked wonderingly at the side of the shattered greenhouse which was even worse by daylight. 'I say, that does look a mess. What happened?'

Sarah Jane cleared her throat warningly. Pollock looked round at Tracey who avoided the eyes, his own seeming to look straight through Brendan. This boy was trying to trick him. He and the girl were trying to trick him. Why else had they not talked of what happened last night?

'Well may you ask,' said the Commander. 'You haven't seen a large white dog by any chance? Hereabouts or over by the chapel?'

Sarah Jane heard Brendan draw breath and came in quickly, seeing a diversion in Pollock's question that would give her time to watch and think. 'Chapel?'

'Well, the ruin,' said the Commander pointing beyond the formal garden to the east of the Manor. 'By the river.'

'No,' said Sarah Jane innocently. Pollock turned and looked penetratingly at Brendan. 'You, boy?'

'No, sir,' replied Brendan just as innocently. K9 may look like a dog, he thought, but he jolly wasn't. He was a robot/computer.

The Commander looked from one to the other intently, searchingly. 'George said a dog did this.'

Sarah Jane resisted the impulse to look at Brendan and prayed that he was doing the same and not drawing attention to her. What more positive proof could there be that Tracey had been involved last night since he'd admitted seeing K9?

'Look at it!' went on Pollock with an angry gesture at what remained of the greenhouse. 'If that dog as much as shows its nose I'll let Jasper tear it to pieces.' Jasper growled as if in agreement, salivating copiously, not to say slobbering. Both Sarah Jane and Brendan in their different ways were amused by the thought that Jasper's chances in a contest with K9 were pretty slim but refrained from even a smile. After all, it was no smiling matter.

Sarah Jane looked at Tracey whose eyes remained watchful under slightly lowered lids. It appeared he was content to keep his own counsel but she wasn't going to let him get away with it.

'My guess is,' she said, 'that whoever attacked Brendan did this.' Watching Tracey closely she saw no flicker of reaction to the statement. He'd been expecting it, of course, and had no intention of giving himself away, but his careful passivity betrayed pre-knowledge of the attack.

'What?' said the Commander, startled.

'Brendan was attacked by two men last night.'

Pollock looked at them both in open disbelief. 'Is this true, boy?'

'Do you doubt my word?' said Sarah Jane primly.

'What?' responded the Commander automatically. 'No, of course not! Don't be so touchy!' He shifted his searching eyes to Brendan. 'When did it happen?'

'About seven o'clock, sir.'

'Where?'

'In the house. In the hall.'

'In the house?' Pollock was palpably flabbergasted. 'I can't believe it. Why wasn't I told?'

'I thought it best not to bother you,' said Sarah Jane evenly.

'Best not to bother me!' His voice lifted indignantly. 'I live in the damn place . . . part of it.'

He sounded very much as if he owned the 'damn place',

but Sarah Jane responded sweetly. 'I thought from what you were telling us yesterday that you had enough to worry about.'

The Commander appeared mollified. His voice came down an octave. 'What happened?'

'Sarah was out,' said Brendan. 'I heard something in the hall. Things were knocked over. And when I went out there they jumped me. And then luckily for me . . .' he winced as Sarah Jane stood on his foot, '. . . one ran off and I managed to fight off the other.'

It was plain that Pollock's credulity was still strained. 'How did they get in?' Brendan looked at Sarah Jane.

'We think they must have had a key.'

'A key?'

'It's a thing you open doors with,' said Sarah Jane looking directly at Tracey who didn't so much as blink.

'You can spare me the sarcasm, young woman,' growled the Commander.

'I'm sorry,' said Sarah Jane, 'but you're not the only one who's angry.'

Pollock grunted acceptance of the apology. 'Were you hurt, boy?'

'No, sir.'

'Did you get a look at these specimens?'

'I got a good look at one of them.'

Sarah Jane was watching Tracey like a lynx and he knew it – and she knew he knew it. Deadlock. The Commander went on: 'So you'd recognise him if you saw him again?'

'Oh, yes.'

Without moving her eyes from Tracey, Sarah Jane's peripheral vision told her that Brendan had thrown her the briefest of glances and she could have kicked him. 'Good,' said Pollock. 'Then we must call in the police.'

'I already have,' said Sarah Jane. 'They're sending someone over to take a statement.'

'Oh, good, good,' rumbled the Commander. 'Nasty business. Frightening for you. But – and I don't mind telling you – pretty rare for around here. Not that it makes it any the less frightening, or course. Anything missing?'

'Only Mr Tracey's son,' said Sarah Jane coolly.

'What's that?' muttered Pollock, having had burglary in mind.

'Oh, I'm sorry,' Sarah Jane came in quickly. 'What did I say? My mind was wandering. I missed seeing Peter about this morning. He was so kind yesterday when I arrived.'

Tracey hadn't turned a hair, knowing full well what she was trying to do. Neither the girl nor the boy had named his son when talking about last night and that could mean only one thing, but he wasn't going to be drawn out into the open. Let them find proof if they could. He said, 'He's over to Blandford, Miss, collecting a harrow that was in for repair. I'll expect he'll be gone most of the day. Slow movers, tractors.'

Not like you, thought Sarah Jane. 'No, nothing's missing,' she said brightly to Pollock.

'Good, good, that's something, I suppose. Let's hope the police can get a lead and the insurance company coughs up on the greenhouse.'

Sarah Jane eased close to Tracey. 'What d'you grow in this area?' she asked, keeping the ball in the air with the intention of involving the man.

'Three varieties of winter cabbage,' replied Tracey without an apparent care in the world. He would give nothing away: he had sworn. 'Lettuce in season,' he continued easily. 'We rotate that every ten days . . . plough in what we don't sell.'

Brendan bent down to scoop up a handful of earth and sniffed it. Pollock and Tracey exchanged a questioning look. Even Sarah Jane gently lifted an eyebrow. Brendan prodded the soil in his hand with an already grimy finger and took another sniff.

'Mmm,' he murmured, 'pH of about nine, I'd say. Isn't that too alkaline?'

He saw Sarah Jane's mouth open. He'd agreed to let her do all the talking, but that was about last night. It didn't include K9's soil analysis and the great fun they'd had together with the dirt on the sitting-room carpet. Sarah Jane watched with fascination as Tracey's face was transformed by a focused hatred, his eyes now wide and boring through Brendan.

'What would you suggest,' he snarled, 'a few hundred kilos of ammonium sulphate?'

'Not as much as that,' said Brendan innocently.

'No,' said Tracey so intensely that a purple vein pulsated at his temple. He flung out an arm with a shaking index finger pointing to a distant crop. 'Over there we had a pH of four.' The finger shifted direction. 'Over there it was six.' His arm went through an arc of sixty degrees and the trembling finger was aimed at a fallow field. 'Over there it's as much as eleven.' His arm dropped to his side as if suddenly overtaken by tiredness. His voice also grew tired. 'There's more to growing than science. Try thinking of the timing. There's no formula for that.' He turned from them and stalked away with a muttered, 'I've got work to do.'

Sarah Jane felt a sudden chill as she realised that the man striding away from them would kill for the land on which they all stood. And yet the land wasn't his; wasn't his, that is, by law.

'I'm afraid you've hurt poor George's feelings,' chuckled the Commander. 'There's nothing much he doesn't know about the care of the soil. Don't make the mistake, young feller-me-lad, that it's all in books. Science can't control the elements. At least, not yet.' He pointed, rather as Tracey had done, at a distant fringe of naked trees. 'See that apple orchard over there? Last September, just before we were due to pick, we had a thirteen second hail storm. Thirteen seconds. I stood and counted 'em. Stripped the lot. Seven thousand quid. I stood and watched it. Five hundred quid a second.'

Sarah Jane was impressed. The world had seen worse disasters but she felt for the man. 'Nothing recoverable?' she asked.

'Bruised fruit and all lifted at once.'

'Yes, I see. But weren't you insured?'

'Insured?' he said bitterly. 'You've got to be joking. Act of God.' He looked away into the distance as if reliving the experience. 'There's your copper,' he said. 'Off you go!'

Sarah Jane and Brendan turned to look in the direction

indicated by the Commander's nod of the head. A police car was creeping politely up the drive.

'See you later,' said Sarah Jane as she and Brendan set off.

'Yes,' said Pollock. 'Come on, Jasper. We're going dog hunting.'

Sarah Jane and Brendan exchanged a safe grin on their way to the police car. 'What's with all this pH stuff?' she said, never having taken in much chemistry at school.

'It's the measure of hydrogen concentration,' said Brendan importantly.

'Oh, that's what it is,' said Sarah Jane sarcastically, none the wiser.

9

Brendan is Taken

Peter Tracey looked with disbelief at his father across the table on which lay the remains of an evening meal.

'I can't do it,' he said hollowly.

'You'll do as you're told,' ordered his father.

'I *can't*!'

'You haven't got any choice. The boy saw you. You've nothing to lose and everything to gain.'

Peter was trapped. He knew that. He had to go through with his father's plan or suffer the consequences. He had to face the police or the indescribable dread of the punishment that would be meted out to him by the elemental forces in which he'd been brought up to believe; the ancient faith held by his family for countless generations. But there was another dread that gripped Peter Tracey; a horror he knew he couldn't live with. 'What are you going to do with him?'

Tracey thrust a finger across the table at his son. 'None of your concern.'

'Yes, it is!' said Peter passionately. 'It is!'

'Don't think about it!'

'How can I *not* think about it?'

'There's a greater issue to think about. Greater than him, greater than you, greater than me.' Tracey's voice was low, urgent and his eyes alight with fanaticism.

'He's only a kid,' moaned Peter.

'Remember that! Remember he's spoiled, privileged, corrupt. That's what you remember! A thief! A stealer of the soil that is rightfully ours from time immemorial. Remember that and do as you're told.'

Peter sank back and lowered his eyes, no longer able to bear the heat in his father's. He had one last desperate hope. Still with downcast eyes he said: 'If we get caught they'll put us inside.'

His father stretched his mouth into a knowing smile. 'You mean you'll get yourself caught? You'll be safe inside? You know better than that. You'll be no safer in prison. Hecate will seek you out . . . will seek me out . . . and her revenge will be terrible. You know that. Take heart! Take courage! The Great One spared you last night. Be eternally grateful that She has given you another chance.'

Peter had not lifted his eyes. His face crumpled and he began to sob. Father looked at son without compassion, his bounden duty done.

Sarah Jane sat at the desk behind her typewriter trying to work on her magazine article without conspicuous success. She looked sightlessly at the near blank page, her thoughts becoming increasingly entangled with the unprovoked attack on Brendan and the brooding imponderability of Bradleigh Manor. She hadn't touched a key for ten minutes.

With elbows propped on the desk she put her chin in her hands and looked at Brendan slumped on the sofa and nodding over a book. It was time he went to bed. She looked at K9 on the rug before the dying fire and smiled with affection. That assemblage of metal, polymers, micro-chips and circuitry was a constant reminder of that epitome of gallantry, the Doctor. It has been decided that morning in the interests of mutual protection from the slobbering Jasper that K9 should remain activated at all times and only hidden in the kennel when no one was at home, a contingency of the afternoon when Sarah Jane had realised she must do some shopping and had taken Brendan into Sherborne with her after a prolonged search for the MGB which Tracey had made almost inaccessible in the large double garage. It was on their return that Brendan had been the first to miss the canine presence of their synthetic friend and since then K9 had occupied the place of traditional comfort in front of the sitting-room fire. Sarah Jane's smile widened as her restless mind dwelt for a moment on the anomaly.

The telephone shrilled, startling Sarah Jane, bringing Brendan fully awake and causing K9's 'ears' to twitch in its direction. Sarah Jane picked up the handset to hear the unmistakable voice of Commander Pollock. 'Good evening, m'dear.'

'Commander Pollock.'

'Just checking that you were both all right.' At the end of the line the Commander was standing in his living-room, still in his overcoat, with his back to the open door. 'I've just got back from my weekly stint with the Sea Scouts in Yeovil and was a bit worried about you.'

Sarah Jane was agreeable surprised. 'How kind of you,' she said.

Pollock gave voice to a self-deprecating jumble of incomprehensible syllables and then went on to ask. 'Is the boy with you?'

'Yes,' said Sarah Jane.

'Good. Now the last thing I want to do . . .' He broke off, hearing a snarl from Jasper. The Alsatian was presenting bare teeth to something beyond the open door.

'Excuse me,' he said. 'Jasper's unhappy about something.' He put down the telephone and went out into the hallway lifting his eyes in seeming self disgust at the sight of the open front door. He moved to close it and went back to the telephone. 'Hello? Sorry about that. I left the front door open. Something you must never do,' he added. 'Now, I don't want you to think that I'm laying down the law or anything like that but I think it's very important you keep an eye on that boy. I don't think you should let him out of your sight, for the time being at least.'

Sarah Jane suddenly became alert, alarmed. 'Have you found out something?'

'No, not yet, but I've been giving this nasty business a lot of thought and I'm liking it less and less. Did you get any help from the police?'

'Well, no,' said Sarah Jane dolefully, 'there's nothing they can do without some sort of evidence, I suppose.'

'No,' agreed the Commander, 'but I'm becoming more and more convinced that this attack on the boy is some sort of personal matter.'

'How do you mean?'

91

'Something to do with your aunt.'

Sarah Jane heard the statement with some relief. Here at last was someone who shared her concern about Aunt Lavinia!

'That's what I'm forced to think,' she confessed.

'Tell me, m'dear . . .' began Pollock and stopped.

'What?' asked Sarah Jane.

'Is there anything you're not telling me?'

Sarah Jane felt sudden alarm. Why should the man ask that? What could he know? 'How d'you mean?' she asked.

'I don't know. It's just an impression I'm getting that you know something I don't.'

Sarah Jane made the decision. 'There is something,' she admitted.

'Ah!'

'But it's something I'd rather not talk about on the phone.'

'Fair enough,' said the Commander briskly. 'I can't come round now. I'm on my way over to Milbourne Port. My sister's poorly and I'm late already. I only dropped back to check you were all right. And I'll probably have to stay the night so what about in the morning, first thing?'

'Yes, all right.'

'Right then. And remember what I said about the boy. Don't let him out of your sight!'

Sarah Jane smiled, feeling the need for a joke. 'There are times when I have to.'

'You know what I mean,' said Pollock with a trace of irritation. 'Don't let him wander about by himself – and bolt the doors before you go to bed.'

'Yes, of course, I'm sorry,' said Sarah Jane contritely.

'Good night, then.'

'Good night, Commander, and thank you.'

Pollock mumbled an acknowledgement and Sarah Jane hung up feeling better than she'd felt all day. 'He's not such a bad old stick.'

'Who? Pollock?' asked Brendan unnecessarily. 'Me no like.'

'Yes,' agreed Sarah Jane, 'and you could make it a little less obvious. You're here for the Christmas holidays, and that's a pretty long time. Anyway, he seems to like you.'

Brendan scoffed. 'Me? You must be joking!'

Sarah Jane stabbed a finger at the telephone. 'Just said so – as good as. Said I shouldn't let you out of my sight. That's the joke.'

'What was he ringing up for?' asked Brendan suspiciously.

'He just wanted to know if we were all right.'

'What didn't you want to talk about on the phone?'

'I thought you were asleep.'

'Well, I wasn't.'

Sarah Jane sighed. She'd have to tell him. 'He's coming round to my way of thinking about Aunt Lavinia. I'm going to tell him about the Tracey's.'

'He's not going to like that,' said Brendan helpfully.

'I know that but I can't see any alternative. They can't be allowed to get away with it. I'm going to tell him in the morning.'

'Oh, all right,' said Brendan and yawned.

'Isn't it about time you turned in?' asked Sarah Jane.

Of the many things distinctly not to Brendan's liking, being sent to bed was very near the top of the list. 'Just want to finish this chapter,' he said, indicating his book. Sarah Jane grimaced and resumed her sterile stare at the near naked page in her typewriter.

The back door of the Manor opened noiselessly. George Tracey sidled into the hall and gestured with a jerk of his head. Peter followed his father in fearfully, carrying a large coil of sash cord and a small canvas bag. Tracey closed the door carefully and relocked it without making a sound. He then slowly, steadily and silently steered his trembling son across the hall to the foot of the staircase which they began cautiously to mount.

On reaching the first landing Tracey prodded Peter in front of him until they reached a door opposite which the stairs again ascended.

'This one,' hissed Tracey. 'Quietly.' Peter opened the door as bidden and the two men entered the moonlit bedroom. 'Now we wait. You there.' He pointed at a patch of shadow between the window and the door. 'And you can put those down. It may be some time.'

Peter, now in better control of himself, put down the rope and the bag and sat on the floor beside them, his back to the wall. He watched his father's silhouette move and mount a chair to take the electric lamp from the ceiling fitting. 'Now we wait,' whispered his father and disappeared in the dark by the bed.

Far from Brendan finishing the chapter, the chapter had finished him. First the book dropped progressively lower to be followed by his head until both could drop no further. It was when he began to snort that Sarah Jane came out of her reverie.

'Brendan!'

The boy's head came up with a snort of snorts, his glazed eyes behind blinking lids, attempting to focus.

'*Bed!*'

'Yes, all right,' groaned Brendan. His book joined several others on the sofa. 'Are you going to tap away on that thing all night?'

'I've done precious little tapping up till now. Perhaps when you've pushed off I'll be inspired.'

'Ha, ha,' brayed Brendan.

'And make sure the doors are bolted.'

'You can't think he'd try it on again? Not knowing the police have been.'

'That's *just* what I think he'd do.'

'But why?' asked Brendan incredulously.

'Because that's what I'd do.'

'You're potty.'

'From way back. *Off!*'

'But why me?' bleated Brendan for the umpteenth time that day. 'I don't get it.'

'That's what we're going to have to find out. Now, push off, will you?'

'I'm going, I'm going. Good night.'

''Night,' mumbled Sarah Jane, concentrating on her near blank page.

'Good night, K9.'

'Greeting reciprocated,' droned K9.

Brendan went out, closing the door behind him, and began to climb the stairs. Then he stopped, sighed and retraced his steps. He crossed to the front door and pushed home the bolts top and bottom. Then he made his way to the back to give it the same treatment. He flicked his hands together as if relieving them of further responsibility and trudged his way upstairs. As soon as he opened his bedroom door he was aware of smelling something sweet. He felt for the light switch which clicked into place to no effect. He was dragged into the dark and a wet pad was clamped over his mouth and nostrils. He gasped and fought the hands for as long as he was conscious.

'Right, I've got him,' whispered Tracey. 'Open the windows! Quietly!'

Peter Tracey did as he was told, opening all three windows gently, leaning heavily on the mullions, bothered himself by the ether fumes. By the light of a small electric torch Tracey put the pad and the bottle back into the canvas bag from which he took a four inch deep strip of elastoplast. This he pressed firmly over Brendan's mouth after first pulling the lips tightly together. 'Hold him!' he ordered. Peter came from the windows to support Brendan while Tracey looped the sash cord about his inert ankles. After being made fast the cord was fed along to Brendan's wrists. These bound, the cord pinioned the arms before being looped under the armpits to form a halter.

'So far, so good,' whispered Tracey triumphantly. 'You see?' Peter's large eyes, in the diffused light of the torch, held nothing but sadness. He let Brendan's trunk down gently onto the floor and his father switched off the torch. 'Now we wait again.'

'Oh dear, K9,' said Sarah Jane heavily.

'Mistress?'

'Just, oh dear.' She released herself from the accusing stare of the near blank page and moved to the sofa where she picked up the book that had sent Brendan to sleep. Its lurid jacket proclaimed it to be the *Encyclopaedia of Witchcraft*. She sat down on the sofa and began to flip through it. 'Well, well,' she muttered. She discarded the book and fingered the four others lying with it: volumes on demonology, the occult, primitive belief. 'All on witchcraft,' she said aloud. 'The little devil! Where did he get this lot, I wonder?'

'Base shelves in north elevation,' announced K9 unexpectedly, quite startling Sarah Jane since she had been talking to herself. It took her a second or two to appreciate the logic of K9's statement and then she was puzzled by the points of the compass. Where on Earth was north? K9, whose eyes were concentrated on Sarah Jane, seemed to read her thoughts. 'I will navigate, Mistress,' he added turning on his axis and gliding towards a book-lined wall. He stopped at a heavy leather armchair that had been placed in an improbable position against the bookshelves. 'Behind obstruction,' indicated the robot.

'Thanks, K9,' said Sarah Jane, heaving the chair aside. In front of her on the three lowest shelves, with gaps made by Brendan's choice, was a small library of works on witchcraft and the occult. Odd, thought Sarah Jane, why all hidden behind a chair like that? And the chair was quite out of place there, anyway.

She gave up. It was all too much for one day. 'Come on, K9,' she said. 'Beddibyes.' With a glance at the dying fire she turned off the lamps and then the light switch at the door. With K9 at her heels she checked that both doors were bolted and went into the kitchen. The cupboard door was opened and K9 glided obediently into his kennel for the night.

'Good night, K9.'

'Greeting reciprocated.'

Sarah Jane wrinkled her pert nose in distaste. 'K9, do me a favour, will you?'

'Mistress?'

'D'you mind making it "good night"?'

'Good night, Mistress.'

'That's better. I love you like a sister, but the pedantry gets on my nerves, all right?'

'Protest duly recorded,' said K9.

'Oh, put a sock in it for Pete's sake,' spluttered Sarah Jane.

'Regret nether hose unavailable,' droned K9.

'That does it!' muttered Sarah Jane and closed the cupboard door impatiently. Enough was enough. She smiled to herself all the way up the stairs. She was tired, worried, unproductive. Poor K9!

On the first landing she switched off the hall light and crossed to Brendan's room. Without opening the door she said: 'Brendan, are you all right?' There being no answer, she repeated the question a little louder. Inside the room Peter whimpered in terror and his father pushed a rough hand over his mouth.

Sarah Jane opened the door. 'Brendan?' she called softly. Tracey yawned audibly, expelled air through his open mouth and then made several small guttural noises. Sarah Jane smiled and closed the door softly.

An hour later, Tracey and his son carried Brendan to the windows relying only on the light of the moon. The bound and gagged boy was manoeuvred into position and left to dangle outside the windows while Peter was lowered on another line looped round a mullion. The line went slack as Peter's feet met the ground and Tracey snaked the line up. He then lowered Brendan in the same manner letting go the line when the tension left it. Then he tossed out the canvas bag, which was caught by Peter, and lowered himself to the ground on a free line which he then twitched clear of the mullion.

In the distance a vixen screeched. Sarah Jane half opened her eyes, turned over and went to sleep.

10

K9 Goes Undercover

Sarah Jane looked at her watch, finished her tea and got up from the kitchen table. K9, liberated from his kennel and at his adopted place by the stove, eased out of her way. She lifted the lid of the frying pan and looked at the brown, buckled bacon, the even browner fried bread, and the two egg yolks which had disappeared behind dry, opaque clouds. She bounced out of the kitchen to the foot of the stairs for the third time and shouted, 'Brendan, you lazy brat, get down here!'

She was halfway back to the kitchen before she remembered that she'd not even heard him in the bathroom. She turned back, sprinted up the stairs and pounded along the landing. If this was the intended pattern of the school holiday it was going to be redrawn instantly. Not bothering to knock she marched into Brendan's bedroom.

The bed hadn't been slept in and the windows were wide open. With a violent change of mood she rushed to the windows and looked down on the trampled flowerbeds beneath.

'Brendan!' she shouted, but this time anger had been overtaken by a terrible fear. She rushed from the room and down the stairs to the sitting-room where she pounced upon the telephone, glancing at the Commander's number written on a pad. With the handset to her ear she'd dialled two digits before realising that the line was dead.

'Wouldn't it be, wouldn't it be!' she muttered in fear and fury and dashed out to the kitchen. Forgetting K9's existence she snatched up her unwieldy bunch of keys and ran to the front door to let herself out.

With a painful stitch in her side she raced round the north-east corner of the house to the main door of the east wing and rang the bell knowing, as she did so, that it wouldn't be answered. If the Commander was back from his sister's he would have called in by now. She wasted no time. She tore back to the kitchen out of breath and in a dire panic. To get to the police she'd have to drive to West Norton and something told her that such a move would be taking her away from Brendan. She knew what she had to do. She would go directly to the man she knew to be responsible. Then she thought of K9. She moved to the cupboard and opened it. 'Right, K9, inside.'

'Negative,' came the unexpected response.

'Negative!' said Sarah Jane indignantly. 'I've got to go out! Inside!'

'Negative.'

'Now, listen you . . .' She was stuck for a suitable epithet. There aren't many terms of abuse attributable to mechanical dogs. She was spared the need, however, for K9 launched into full cry. 'From observation make assumption: Brendan missing, telephone out of order, Commander Pollock not available.'

Sarah Jane had to sit down. She did so at the kitchen table and looked at K9 hard. She'd forgotten about him, underestimated him. She was filled with a mixture of relief and admiration. How could her predicament have been better expressed?

'I'm sorry, K9,' she said simply.

'Sorrow unnecessary, action imperative,' said K9.

Sarah Jane would never again repeat the mistake of forgetting that K9 was a friend, an ally, an extension of the Doctor himself. 'What action, K9?' she asked.

'Confront the man Tracey.'

Excitement took hold of Sarah Jane. An ally indeed! 'That's just what I was going to do,' she almost shouted as she jumped out of her chair. 'So, into the cupboard, dear K9.'

'Negative. Imperative I accompany, Mistress.'

'But that's impossible, K9. You'll be seen, and then what will happen? It's too risky.'

'Greater risk for Mistress to face Tracey alone. Animal at bay most dangerous.'

Sarah Jane knew K9 to be right. From what Brendan had told her about the stunning of Peter Tracey the robot had formidable powers that had to be acknowledged. But for them both to be seen together in broad daylight? Sooner of later, she supposed, K9 would have to be revealed to a wondering world but not now, not until the implied violence of the present situation had been dealt with finally and irrevocably.

'K9,' she said solemnly, 'you're not only a gift from the Doctor, you've already become a true friend and I'll be hanged if I'm going to have you exposed to whatever wickedness is going on here. You could finish up in some scrap metal yard and I know I couldn't bear that.' She suddenly became conscious that she was being terribly sentimental. 'All right, speech over,' she said harshly. 'You're the brains, K9. You accompany me to see Tracey and he sees you. What then?'

'Not necessary for me to be seen,' said K9.

'Oh,' said Sarah Jane remembering her resolve never again to underestimate him, 'you mean you can make yourself invisible?'

'Negative, but Mistress can.'

'*Me* invisible?' said an astonished Sarah Jane.

'Negative. Suggest carriage in portable container.'

'Portable container?'

'Such as brought yesterday.'

Sarah Jane suddenly twigged. Her luggage dumped by K9's packing-case on her arrival. 'My holdall!'

'Holdall capacious enough,' confirmed K9.

'Don't go away!' gasped Sarah Jane racing from the kitchen and up the stairs. In her room she up-ended the holdall, shedding the contents over the bed and hurried back to the kitchen with it. She put the lip of the bag on the floor, stretching it flush. K9 was able to track into the holdall. Sarah Jane hefted it a few inches from the floor to allow K9 to settle, grateful that the robot seemed less heavy than she remembered when trying to get him out of his packing-case. She put the holdall down again and crowned the joint effort with a kitchen towel. K9 was invisible.

Sarah Jane and K9 didn't have far to go. Tracey's cottage had been pointed out to her the day before when she had been having trouble finding where the man had parked her car. It was near the shop: an early seventeenth-century dwelling of considerable charm and character, cob built under a thatched roof. Sarah Jane was grateful for a chance to put the holdall down; something she'd avoided doing on the way from the Manor in case some watching eye became curious about the weight she was carrying.

The cottage door could have been the one which had been hung when the place was built. It had a wooden latch fastening, a mortise lock and an anomalous electric bell button which Sarah Jane pushed. With no answer to her second ring she tried the latch and the door opened.

She pushed in boldly and adjusted her eyes to the dim interior. The living-room was agreeable, comfortable but predictably neglected and untidy. She called loudly, 'Anyone at home?' Her voice laughed back at her. She crossed to the foot of the stairs ascending directly from the room. 'Anybody up there?' She wasn't surprised the place was empty. Tracey was hiding, she knew that. But hiding in his work, inaccessible somewhere on the soil he cared for, visiting a distant destination on a slow tractor. She strode outside, closed the door and picked up the holdall.

'Mistress.' K9's voice was muffled. Sarah Jane looked about her quickly and put K9 down.

'What?' she asked softly.

'Leave me here!'

'Leave you here?'

'Affirmative.'

Sarah Jane thought for a moment. 'What have you got in mind?' adding, as she pondered the accuracy of the noun in relation to a complex of electronics, 'so to speak.'

'Request access to interior.'

True to her earlier promise to herself concerning K9's acumen, Sarah Jane took another quick look round, picked up the holdall, re-entered the living-room and put K9 down. 'Right. Now what?'

'Request removal from holdall.'

101

Sarah Jane removed the kitchen towel and eased the hold-all onto its side while keeping the robot propped in a perpendicular position. K9 tracked himself out onto the stone-flagged floor, revolved on his axis through three hundred and sixty degrees and disappeared behind a comfortable-looking sofa. Sarah Jane waited.

'Come on, K9, I've no time to muck about.'

'Will report after dark, Mistress.'

Sarah Jane thought about this. Leave him here for seven hours or more? Would he be safe? Another glance round the room confirmed that Tracey had little time for house work and that the sofa probably hadn't been moved since it was bought; and it would be a great tactical advantage to have a spy planted in the enemy camp for so long. No, it was too risky.

'Come on out, K9!'

'Negative!'

'No, K9, it's too risky.'

'Negative,' repeated K9 implacably.

'All right,' agreed Sarah Jane. 'So you stay here until dark. What happens then?'

'Mistress will think of something.'

Sarah Jane was quite chuffed. 'That's flattery indeed, coming from you,' she said.

'Flattery ineffectual persuader,' droned the hidden K9.

Why, you little devil, thought Sarah Jane, what else are you using to get round me? She knew that a silicon chip synthesis could be considerably more stubborn than a mule and that she was physically incapable of winkling a rebellious robot out from behind that sofa. She sighed. 'All right,' she said, 'have it your way. But be careful. And good luck,' she added.

'Superstition illogical and self-destructive,' responded K9.

Oh, tish! thought Sarah Jane and, picking up her holdall, she flounced out. There was no one in sight in the shop or on the open land of the market garden so far as she could see and, taking some comfort in this, she hurried across the drive to where it forked for access to the garages. A car horn sounded an urgent tattoo of three blasts and she stopped and turned to see a green Range Rover coming up the drive from the road. Sarah Jane was running to Pollock before he pulled up.

'Brendan's missing,' she gasped.

'What!'

'His bed's not been slept in. The windows were wide open and the flowerbeds underneath trampled down.'

'I don't believe it!'

'It's true. What's more the phone's dead. I'm going to the police.'

'Hop in!' said the Commander, 'we'll go together.' He leaned over to open the near side door and Sarah Jane clambered up into the seat beside him, pitching her holdall into the back. Jasper, semi-supine on the back seats, growled unpleasantly, sniffed the holdall and went back to sleep. Pollock reversed, turned out through the Manor gates and drove through the village heading east. 'Another break-in,' he said, 'I can't believe it. The doors were bolted?'

'Oh, yes,' said Sarah Jane, her breathing steadying. 'But they didn't come in that way. They got in through his window. Like all kids, he's careless.'

'They?'

'George Tracey and his son Peter,' said Sarah Jane.

The Commander drove on in silence until they were clear of Hazelbury Abbas. 'Is this what you couldn't tell me on the phone?' he asked.

'Yes.'

'I see.' He was again silent for some time and Sarah Jane couldn't dismiss the feeling that he shared her suspicions. She remembered his concern for Brendan the night before and his opinion that the motive behind the attack in some way involved Aunt Lavinia.

'Why didn't you tell me this before?' Pollock asked eventually.

Sarah Jane hesitated, in some embarrassment. 'I'm afraid I'm a bit mixed up,' she admitted. 'I didn't want to upset anybody . . . for Aunt Lavinia's sake. And I liked what I'd seen of Peter. Brendan came to no harm and you . . . well, you have a reputation for being rather harsh.'

'A bit different now, though, isn't it?' he said, smiling tightly.

'Yes,' Sarah Jane had to own, 'it's a bit different now.'

The Range Rover sped through Haddon Parva, its driver disregarding the speed limit. 'Have you got any proof?' asked Pollock.

'Proof?'

'If you're going to repeat this accusation to the police you'll need to have some proof.'

'Brendan described Peter. The police already have the description.'

'Yes, I see. Fair enough. But what about his father?'

'Brendan didn't see him, only Peter. But I'm convinced his father's behind all this.'

'Yes,' sighed the Commander. 'The trouble is we've got to convince the police.' He drove into West Norton and turned up Longacres. 'I must tell you, m'dear, that I don't like the sound of any of this. We'll never replace George. They don't come any better.'

Sarah Jane didn't like the sound of any of that either. 'I'm not sure what you're saying, Commander.'

'I'm saying the police have got a description of Peter and that's all.'

Sarah Jane felt a mounting anger. This man was going to surrender principle to self-interest and protect Tracey! 'Are you defending George Tracey?'

'No, I'm not,' said Pollock evenly. 'Far from it. If he's responsible for Brendan's disappearance he'll pay the penalty. And I shall be the first to see that he does. Just be careful what you say to the police. George has good friends hereabouts and there's such a thing as defamation.'

Sarah Jane was mollified.

The Range Rover turned from Longacres into Trentgate Square, an enclosed area dominated by the church with a number of shops testifying to the imminence of Christmas. The Commander pulled up opposite the church and in front of West Norton police station, a converted fourteenth century terrace dwelling said to have once been a house of correction. It was a sub-station comprising, beyond a small reception area, not more than an interview room, an office and a kitchenette. As Pollock, in courtly fashion, opened the near side door of the Rover to help Sarah Jane to the pavement she said, 'Did Aunt Lavinia and Tracey quarrel in any way?'

'Not that I know of,' said the Commander. 'Not your aunt's way. She let us get on with things without the slightest interference. Nothing to quarrel about there,' and he opened the door of the station and gestured that Sarah Jane should precede him.

PC Carter considered himself lucky to have visited Bradleigh Manor since it had introduced him to a pretty newcomer of his own age. You couldn't expect much of that around here.

'Miss Smith! Good morning! Good morning, Commander.'

'Morning,' grumbled Pollock.

'My phone's out of order . . .' began Sarah Jane.

'I'm sorry, Miss Smith,' interrupted Carter, 'but I'm afraid in the time we've had . . .'

'Brendan's now missing.'

'Missing?'

At a desk behind Carter sat a sergeant listening at a telephone. He half-turned as Sarah Jane blurted out, 'Disappeared. And I believe the man who's behind it . . .'

It was Pollock's turn to interrupt. 'Steady now,' he warned quietly. Sarah Jane threw him a sidelong glance, saying, 'I believe a man called Peter Tracey . . . who lives at the Manor . . . has something to do with it.'

This announcement caused great embarrassment in the fledgling PC Carter who turned, as if for help, to his superior on the telephone. 'I'll call you back,' said the sergeant into the receiver. He hung up and rose to join Carter at the counter.

'Morning, Wilson,' grunted Pollock.

'Good morning, Commander,' greeted Sergeant Vince Wilson. There was no way for Sarah Jane to know that she was face to face with a witch, a member of the coven that had

105

celebrated the esbat at the last full moon.

'Miss Smith, Sarge,' introduced Carter, 'about the boy who was attacked the . . .'

'I heard,' said Wilson. 'How long's he been missing?'

'Since last night,' said Sarah Jane.

'Did he go out somewhere?'

'No, he didn't. Not of his own accord,' said Sarah Jane firmly. 'The doors front and back were bolted from the inside.'

Wilson looked from Sarah Jane to the Commander and back again uncomfortably. 'Is there any evidence of a break-in elsewhere?'

'Funny you should ask that,' said Sarah Jane tartly. 'His windows were open and the flowerbeds underneath trampled on.'

Wilson was even more uncomfortable. 'What makes you think Peter Tracey was involved?'

Sarah Jane looked incredulously from Sergeant Wilson to PC Carter. 'Doesn't he fit Brendan's description?'

PC Carter looked unhappily at Sergeant Wilson and Sergeant Wilson looked unhappily at Commander Pollock. 'This is a tricky one, Commander.'

'Yes,' agreed Pollock. He looked contemplatively at Sarah Jane and then away again, clearly considering a painful course of action. Having made up his mind, he looked at Sarah Jane squarely.

'I'm sorry, m'dear, but what you didn't know – but will have to know now – is that Peter's got a suspended sentence . . . six months ago. Housebreaking. In a sense he's in his father's custody.'

The information came to Sarah Jane more as a relief than a shock. 'Then what are you waiting for?' she asked.

Wilson looked apologetic. 'Peter's also missing. His father came to us last night.'

'Oh, no!' said the Commander in exasperation, 'don't tell me the kid's absconded!'

'We don't know, sir,' said Wilson. 'Only that his father came to us for help . . . very worried.'

'And he's not the only one,' said Sarah Jane emphatically.

106

She looked from one to the other in hurt bewilderment and anger. 'What's going on here? My aunt goes off mysteriously. Then Brendan's attacked . . . and then he disappears. What's the matter with this place?'

There was no question that Wilson's concern was genuine. In fact, did Sarah Jane but know, his concern was far greater than hers.

'Try not to worry, Miss,' he said. 'We'll put out a general alert. The wisest thing for you do do is to stay where we can reach you.'

Sarah Jane fumed. 'Right,' she snapped. And again: 'Right!'

PC Carter watched her go miserably. 'Shall I do the alert, Sarge?'

Wilson turned to look at Carter dully. 'Yes,' he said dispiritedly, 'you do that.'

Sarah Jane was still fuming when she reached the Range Rover. 'What now?' she asked grimly as Pollock settled into his seat. 'I don't know,' said the Commander, 'But I want to talk to George Tracey.'

'You'll be lucky!'

The Commander turned to look at her. 'Temper,' he said gently.

'Sorry.'

'Who knows, I may be luckier than you.' He saw someone approach from the direction of the church with a grunt of displeasure. Sarah Jane turned to find Lily Gregson, in her Sunday best, smiling at her through the glass but was in no mood to lower the window.

'Hello, dear!' called Lily. 'Good morning, Commander.'

'Morning,' groaned Pollock.

Lily tapped on the window with her prayer book in the expectation that it be wound down. Sarah Jane relented. The post mistress beamed at her through the open window. 'Have you heard from your Auntie?'

'No, not yet.' Sarah Jane felt like adding that no word from her aunt was now the lesser of her worries but was too depressed.

'Never mind,' went on Lily blithely, 'no news is good news. And if I don't see you before . . . merry Christmas.'

'And to you.'

Sarah Jane wound up the window as Lily walked off, nodding happily to herself. Pollock started up, went into gear and drove off.

'Why does she come to church here?' asked Sarah Jane idly. 'What's wrong with Hazelbury Abbas?'

'The vicar,' said Pollock briefly.

'What's wrong with him?'

'Nothing. Nice enough young feller.'

'Oh, he's young,' realised Sarah Jane aloud.

'And *liberal*. Lily doesn't like the new hymns and the new Bible. She's a traditionalist. Are you a churchgoer?'

'Not as you'd notice,' said Sarah Jane gloomily. 'I go when I can. It's difficult most of the time, trotting about as I do.'

The Commander acknowledged her statement with a typical grunt and it was the only sound to pass between them until they reached the Manor. Sarah Jane collected her hold-all with her thoughts firmly on K9. She felt lonely, in need of someone, something, other than Pollock to confide in. And perhaps Tracey had come back. Perhaps K9 would already have something to report.

Pollock stopped near the empty shop, a short distance from the Tracey cottage. 'All right,' he said, 'we'll see him together.'

'He's not in,' said Sarah Jane, thinking of K9.

'You mean he *wasn't* in,' growled the Commander, on his way to the cottage. Sarah Jane followed quickly, praying that K9 was still out of sight. He was. At the foot of the stairs Pollock shouted: 'George!'

'Perhaps he's asleep?' suggested Sarah Jane in the forlorn hope that the Commander would investigate and allow her a quick check on K9.

'At this time in the morning?'

'It *is* Sunday.'

'Doesn't mean a thing to George. He'll be looking for Peter or he's gone over to see his mother at Beaminster.'

Or on a slow tractor to Land's End, thought Sarah Jane.

Outside Pollock nodded at the Range Rover. 'Like me to drop you off?'

'No, thanks. It's no distance.'

The Commander eyed the holdall. 'Can't think what you're humping that around for. Empty, isn't it?'

Sarah Jane attempted a laugh. 'Silly, isn't it? I thought I'd do some shopping. I'd forgotten it was Sunday. I'm afraid that's the sort of state I'm in.'

'Mmm,' grunted the Commander. 'Shouldn't be on your own, brooding. You're welcome to a cup of coffee in my place if you've a mind.'

Sarah Jane was touched. 'That's more than kind of you,' she said, 'but I'll have a go at some work. That'll help.'

'Please yourself,' Pollock said gruffly. 'I'll report your telephone and call round if I hear anything.'

'Thanks.' She walked unhurriedly to the Manor waiting for the Range Rover to move out of sight. Then, with a quick look around, she doubled back to the cottage and ducked through the door.

'K9?'

'Mistress?'

'Are you all right?'

'Affirmative.'

'Anything to report?'

'Negative.'

'I've been to the police. They know nothing. I thought you'd want to know.'

'Mistress,' acknowledged K9.

'I'll go now,' said Sarah Jane reluctantly. 'See you later.'

'Affirmative, Mistress.'

Sarah Jane let herself out of the cottage cautiously, half-expecting to meet Tracey returning home. She had remembered K9's words about her confronting alone: animal at bay most dangerous.

She needn't have worried. Hidden between the confined walls of a disused brick furnace, Tracey watched her walk towards the Manor from a safe distance.

11

Human Sacrifice

Sarah Jane had torn the taunting near-blank page from her typewriter, screwed it savagely into a ball and banged it into the waste paper basket. She looked at her watch. That had been six hours ago. It was now five o'clock and it had been dark for an hour. What was she going to do about K9? The virgin white sheet in her typewriter gleamed at her mockingly.

She got up and moved about the sitting-room restlessly, wondering just how many miles she must have covered in it during the day. She picked up the handset of the telephone. Still dead. She went to the fire and poked the logs onto their unburnt sides watching the sparks fly and new flames flare. She'd had nothing to eat all day and was cold; unhungry but cold.

'Oh, Brendan, where the devil are you!' she moaned.

Brendan was also cold. Reasonably comfortable on his bed of hay, but cold. He said so.

'I'm sorry,' said Peter Tracey, 'so am I. They won't let us have a stove because of the hay.'

'Who's they?' asked Brendan for perhaps the tenth time. Peter was silent. 'All right, then, why can't we have the torch on? It might feel warmer.'

'The battery'll run down.'

'Well, let it run down. What're you saving it for?'

A click preceded a beam from a car torch lighting up the interior of the hay barn. Brendan lay on a bank of loose hay by a number of tight bales. He was wrapped in a rough blanket and his wrists were tied. He's grown tired of asking what they were doing here and why. He'd been asking since he regained consciousness that morning. And he'd asked the elderly, melancholy man, with long hair and beard, who'd brought them something to eat and drink at midday. But the melancholy gaoler had said nothing as he superintended the meal, retied Brendan's wrists, and took himself off with the plates and cider mugs.

Brendan looked at Peter also huddled in a blanket and propped against bales a few feet away. 'Your father's mad, that's about the size of it, isn't it?' Peter said nothing. 'He must be to treat you like this.'

'*Shut up!*' said Peter savagely.

After a while Brendan said, 'What about putting some more of this hay on me? That'd be warmer.'

Peter got to his feet and covered the boy with a generous layer of loose hay. 'I still feel sick,' said Brendan.

'You're all right.'

'How d'you know I'm all right? You don't know how I feel. It's that stuff you put me out with, isn't it?'

'You're all right,' insisted Peter. 'Somebody came out from the hospital to see you.'

'A doctor?'

'He said you'd be all right when you'd had something to eat.'

'You mean a doctor's been here? What's going on? That's what I want to know. What's going on?' Peter went back to his place saying nothing. 'Well, I've had something to eat and I still feel awful. Perhaps I wouldn't feel so bad if my hands weren't tied. Why are my hands tied and not yours?' Peter said nothing. 'Come on, untie me why don't you?'

'You tied mine,' hissed Peter.

'Yes, I did. I was frightened.'

'So am I.'

'Frightened of me?' said Brendan derisively. He waited in vain for an answer. 'I suppose you know what's going to happen to you and your father when I get out of here, don't you?'

Brendan couldn't clearly see his fellow prisoner who was behind the beam of the torch but he could hear him, and what he was listening to was sobbing. He continued to listen for a moment in wonderment. 'Peter,' he said quietly, after a

111

while, 'what's the matter?'

'Oh, shut up!' choked Peter through his tears. '*Shut up! Shut up! Shut up!*'

'Well, I must say!' muttered Brendan indignantly.

The long silence after that was broken by muffled voices and a scraping against wood as a batten was lifted outside the barn door. Hinges creaked and a man's voice, well modulated and unrecognised by Brendan, said, 'Right, Peter, you're wanted, and bring the torch.'

Peter got up and did as he was bidden, going out of sight with the light of the torch. The hinges protested again, the door banged and the batten was dropped into position.

'Hey, wait a minute!' yelled Brendan. 'You're not going to leave me alone in here without a light! What about the rats?'

'They won't harm you,' answered the voice, 'if you don't harm them.'

'Come back!' shrieked Brendan. 'Come back here!'

'And shout as loud and as long as you like,' the voice went on reassuringly, 'no one can hear you.'

Sarah Jane let the curtain fall back into place and turned from the window. The moon was already quite high and nearly full. She'd have little trouble picking her way since she'd covered the ground to the cottage often enough but it could be another matter getting K9 out of there.

'Mistress will think of something,' K9 had said. Well, Mistress hadn't thought of something. Mistress hadn't a thought in her tiny head. It was all very well for K9 to shift the responsibility for his rescue to her but he was the one with the brains. He'd said so himself. All she could do was to go to the cottage and hope it was in darkness. But supposing it wasn't? Suppose Tracey was now at home? Part of her willed this to be so since it would increase K9's chances of learning something but how was she to get K9 out from under Tracey's nose? And another thing: Tracey had this habit of leaving his front door unlocked during the daytime but what if he locked it at night as he was almost bound to do? K9 would be trapped all night with no chance of learning anything that might help Brendan.

There was nothing else for it. She'd have to play this one by ear. She got the torch from the kitchen and collected her leather jacket and the holdall from the hall. Leaving the lights on to suggest she was still at home, she went out stealthily by the back door, locking it behind her.

She made her way slowly and vigilantly to the cottage, making no noise. Her heart sank: lights were on. She sat down on an upturned box in the shadow of a lean-to at the shop, resigning herself to a long wait. Then she noticed something that made her less pessimistic. Leaning against a wall by the cottage door was a bicycle, a man's bicycle. She'd never seen one there before and never seen Tracey use one. Could it mean that he had a visitor?

Sergeant Vince Wilson's steady, wide-apart eyes accepted the challenge in Tracey's fanatical stare. 'Where *is* the boy?'

'I'll not tell you.'

'You don't need to. I can guess,' said Wilson heavily. 'This can't be. It's madness! It's criminal!'

'It's survival,' rapped back Tracey.

'No,' said Wilson. 'Not at that price!'

'You are bound.'

Wilson needed no reminder of this. The conflict within him was the greatest torment he could remember. He was bound by his faith, by his oath, true. But he was also bound by something else: his duty as a public servant, to say nothing of his humanity. He had to fight to reverse this insane decision. 'It's madness, I tell you!'

There was malice in the set of Tracey's lips. 'Are you saying the All Highest are mad?'

Wilson knew his opponent was tempting him into blasphemy. It was a trap he had no intention of falling into. 'There hasn't been a human sacrifice since 1791.'

'The order is abroad. You're bound by your oath.'

'I'm also a policeman.'

'Hecate's law is higher. You know that very well. And the Almighty One has warned us. She sent her familiar . . . the white dog . . . to warn us. Be warned!' Tracey's voice trembled. 'Unless She is obeyed She will destroy us all. She will take our lives and then our immortal souls!'

Wilson knew this to be ultimate truth. That cosmic forces ruled the Universe was self-evident and irrefragable, however stridently the new religions denied this. In the beginning was cosmic force and so it would remain forever, untouched by the puniness of mankind that, in its ignorance and stupidity and, above all, vanity, anthropomorphised its gods. The occult was the only true communion. And yet there were those of his faith who clung tenaciously to primitive extremes, repudiating the liberalising influence of the civil law just as those of the Christian faith clung fervently to the practice of ritual cannibalism. Tracey was one of these. So, too, were the All Highest who led the coven. Wilson made up his mind. He was bound by his oath but that didn't prevent him from interceding on behalf of the boy and upholding the law of the land. Sanity must prevail. He turned to the door.

'Where are you going?' demanded Tracey.

'Guess!' said Wilson and was gone.

'You'll not get to Halstock!' shouted Tracey. Adding quietly as he reached for the telephone, 'I'll see to that.'

Sarah Jane saw the sergeant leave the cottage with a surprise which was closely followed by hope. Had he come to Tracey with news of his son? Had he, perhaps, something to tell her? She got to her feet and was on the point of calling out when she remembered Tracey and the trapped K9. She watched in silence as Wilson reached his bicycle and wheeled it hurriedly towards the road. She sat down again to wait. At least there would be something for K9 to report. She hadn't to wait long. Tracey came out of his cottage in a rush leaving the lights on and the door open. Sarah Jane watched him out of sight and hurried through the door. 'K9?' she said urgently.

'Mistress.'

'Come on! Out of there before he gets back.' As K9 came out from behind the sofa she stretched the lip of the holdall tight to the flagstones inviting him to enter.

'No time, Mistress,' said K9 tracking through the door. 'Request follow.'

'Now, hang about!' protested Sarah Jane.

'Request follow,' insisted K9.

Sergeant Wilson, pedalling fast, turned left after Knighton Maybank heading south. It would have been quicker to go back to West Norton and get a car but that would attract an explanation for its official use and this he was bound not to give. He panted with the exertion of pushing his large frame along the incline to Stoford. The solstice sabbat was two days off. He hadn't got a lot of time.

K9 had led the way to the comparative safety of an outhouse, adjacent to the closed shop, where the wire baskets used by the customers were stored.

'Mistress?' intoned K9 interrogatively.

Sarah Jane stood in the dark, supported by the wall at her back, rigid with shock. What K9 had reported was of un-believable horror: that Tracey and Wilson were witches and that Brendan was to be a human sacrifice! The blood pounded at her throat and temples and her mouth was bone dry.

'Mistress?' repeated K9.

'I can't think,' got out Sarah Jane hoarsely. 'I can't think, I can't think! Help me, K9, help me!'

'Advise pursuit,' said K9.

'Pursuit?'

'Pursuit of policeman.'

'Don't be so stupid!' snapped Sarah Jane. 'I don't even know where he's going. And even if . . .'

'Halstock,' snapped back K9.

'Halstock?'

'Affirmative.'

She'd heard that name before. But where and from whom? It didn't matter. Now that she knew where Wilson was going there was a good chance she could catch him up and join forces since K9 had reported Wilson's repugnance of the abomination proposed for Brendan. But first she must get word to the Commander.

'Mistress.'

'Yes!' bit back Sarah Jane, irritated that her new flow of thought was being interrupted.

'Possibility policeman in need of assistance.'

'What?'

'Tracey telephoned interception.'

'Telephoned who? Do you know?'

'Negative.'

Sarah Jane abandoned all thought of calling in the Commander and raced for the garages. 'Come on, K9! And don't hang about! If you're seen you're seen and that's that.'

With the moon fitfully shining between drifting clouds, Sergeant Wilson crossed the long bridge before Sutton Bingham at speed and pedalled steadily down the straight stretch of narrow road bordering the reservoir. He was less than a mile from Halstock.

Just before a turn to the right signposted Gorscombe a cloud smudged out the moon. An eerie light played on the bare trees ahead giving them an uncanny movement: an encirclement, a closing in. Wilson slowed down. He'd known this stretch of road all his life but he knew of no source of light such as this. It certainly didn't originate from a car. Suddenly a shrill sound burst from the bank to his left and the policeman pulled up. The sound, like the bleating of a large goat, began to gain in volume. 'No,' moaned Wilson, his eyes wide with horror. 'No, no, no, no, no!'

The bleating reached demonic proportions.

Sarah Jane had tucked K9 into the back of the MGB, checked the shortest route to Halstock with the aid of the torch and put her foot well down in high hopes of overtaking Wilson. Although still sick with anxiety her head was clearer now that she had a possible explanation of the mysteries concerning Bradleigh Manor and a positive plan of action. She'd listened to K9's verbatim account of Wilson's confrontation with Tracey, droned at her from the back of the car, and found herself mentally drafting a piece that could possibly make plausible the astonishing anomaly of a policeman practicing witchcraft. She came back to the matter in hand. 'Water to

116

the left, K9,' she said.

'Sutton Bingham reservoir,' was K9's response, his probe
scanning the map in the light of the torch. Sarah Jane was
afflicted by a curious neurosis when driving which amounted
to an unreasonable fear of losing the way. She had a profound
distrust of signposts which indicated that her destination lay
to the left when she knew, without doubt, that it lay to the
right. She drove by the compass which bore little relation to a
local authority's layout of highways. K9 had been instructed
to navigate. The high beam of the MGB showed a signpost.
'Right turn ahead, K9, reading Garscombe.'

'Proceed present direction,' instructed K9.

All very well, thought Sarah Jane, but there's something in
the road. She slowed the car and came to a halt a matter of feet
from the fallen bicycle. She knew instantly it was Wilson's
even before she saw the policeman collapsed on the road a few
yards in front of his machine. She knew too, as she left the car
and hurried to him, that she was already too late. Vince
Wilson lay on his back, his helmet free of his head and
rocking mockingly in the light wind. In the sudden, un-
clouded light of the near-full moon his eyes and mouth were
wide open in death. Sarah Jane covered her face with her
hands and moaned. Brendan's only hope had paid a terrible
price for his disaffection.

'Witches? Human sacrifice?' almost squeaked Pollock. He
sat slumped on the sofa in his neglected sitting-room, with
Jasper at his feet, staring in disbelief at Sarah Jane sitting
forward earnestly on the chair in front of him. 'George, and
Vince Wilson?'

'You've got to believe me!' said Sarah Jane desperately.

'You *heard* them?'

'Yes,' she said – after the slightest hesitation.

'You don't seem sure.'

'You've simply got to believe me!' shouted Sarah Jane,
pounding her knee hysterically.

'All right, all right,' said the Commander quickly, 'Where
is he now?'

Sarah Jane was bewildered. 'Who?'

'Wilson.'

'At the hospital. I called an ambulance and the police.'

'What did they say?' asked Pollock keenly.

'That it looked like cardiac arrest due to shock.'

'The police said that?'

'No, the ambulance people.'

'What did the police say?'

Sarah Jane hesitated again. It was all too painful to recall and she knew that time must be running out for Brendan.

'You told them what you've just told me?' went on the Commander. 'Or didn't you?'

Sarah Jane was on the point of tears. 'Yes, I told them.'

'And?'

'I don't think they believed me,' she choked. Pollock looked at her with compassion, watching the girl's hands clench and unclench as she fought to keep control of herself. 'Hardly surprising, is it?' he said gently. 'A police sergeant a witch?'

Sarah Jane looked at him in torment. He was her last chance – Brendan's last chance. 'Do you believe me?' she pleaded. The Commander regarded her steadily for some agonising seconds.

'I've often been told I'm out of my mind,' he said quietly, 'So perhaps I am.' He rose to his feet. 'Yes,' he said simply. 'I believe you.'

Sarah Jane was so flooded with relief and overcome with gratitude she could have hugged him. She bounded up. 'But,' said Pollock raising a hand imperiously like a policeman holding up traffic, 'please don't.'

'Don't what?'

'Do what I think you had it in mind to do.' He put his head on one side and smiled charmingly.

'Oh!' said Sarah Jane with something approaching an answering smile; 'all right, I won't then.'

'That's an improvement,' said the Commander. 'Come on! The state you're in I think you'd better come with me.'

'Where are you going?'

'To Tracey's.'

'I don't think he's in. There was no light on when I came

118

back.'

'I know he's not in. I saw him go out. I have a key. That place is as much an estate office as it is his home. Come on!'

Peter Tracey sat in the half light of the skittle alley behind the public bar of The White Hart. He licked dry lips and his large, frightened eyes flicked from one to another of the ring of familiar faces looking intently at him: Henry Tobias, the newspaper editor; Byron Weekes, the poet and his gaoler at the farm; Michael Barnett, the male nurse from the hospital; John Sterling, the cabinet maker and Rosemary Creach, the midwife. The silence in the alley was intensified by the sounds of conviviality coming from the distant bar, sounds which increased in volume suddenly as Tracey entered with Stanley Shields, the publican, carrying a small tumbler half filled with amber fluid. 'Here, drink this!' said Tracey. Peter shook his head. 'Drink it! It'll calm you down.'

Peter took the glass with a hand shaking so badly that he had to use the other to guide the drink to his lips. He took the liquid in one gulp and coughed. 'Now, pull yourself together! You've always wanted to be let in.' Peter shook his head fiercely. 'It makes no difference. You've been chosen.' The boy moaned and the glass fell from his hands and shattered on the stone floor. 'You'll be initiated tonight.'

Peter lifted his head and let out a cry of pain, tears forming in his wide eyes and spilling to his cheeks. His father jerked his head at John Sterling. The cabinet maker moved to the skittle run and began banging down wood balls at the distant ninepins.

Byron Weekes said, 'If the boy's recalcitrant it makes him dangerous.'

Tracey rounded on the poet. 'He's already bound. He was bound from birth. You know that and he knows it and we must be complete for the solstice.'

Peter Tracey found his voice at last in one long piercing scream. Tracey slapped his son's face hard, silencing the scream but not the tormented moaning that succeeded it. 'It's not easy for a father to acknowledge that his only son is a coward,' Tracey said with quiet ferocity. 'Redeem yourself!

Or go like Vince Wilson to everlasting fire!'

Sarah Jane had joined determinedly in the thorough search the Commander had made of the living-room and kitchen but she had baulked at accompanying him to the rooms upstairs. It was, in any case, unlikely that clues suggesting where Brendan might be hidden would be found up there. She listened, with Jasper, to Pollock moving about above with the crippling fear creeping back that they were already too late to save the unhappy boy.

She wondered if he knew, wherever he was, what horrible fate awaited him and if he had given up hope of being found. Was he, perhaps, pinning his hopes on his hero worship of K9? Should she confide in the Commander about the robot? She rejected the idea. You only got from a computer what had been fed into it, and there was nothing more to be fed in. She resented the thought of K9, tucked away in his kennel, not being able to offer some inspired flash that would dispel the never-ending nightmare. She picked up a framed portrait photograph of a handsome young woman as Pollock came down the stairs.

'Nothing,' he said. 'Not a blessed thing. There wouldn't be, come to think of it.' He looked across at Sarah Jane as she put down the photograph. 'His wife,' he said shortly. 'Spirited woman. A little too spirited. She died in a car crash five years ago. Not far from where you found Wilson, as a matter of fact. Dangerous stretch that. Well, m'dear, I don't know where we go from here.'

'Halstock,' said Sarah Jane firmly.

'Why?'

'Because that's were Brendan is. He must be somewhere there.'

'Why?' repeated Pollock.

'Because that's where Sergeant Wilson said he was going.'

The Commander looked doubtful. 'D'you remember exactly what he said?'

Sarah Jane tried hard to think of K9's exact words. 'He didn't say it. It was Tracey.'

'What did he say then?'

'You'll not get to Halstock.'

'Mmm,' murmured the Commander. 'Halstock's little more than a hamlet. A pub, a few cottages, farmland. Where do we look? And for a house to house search we need the police and a warrant, and there's not a shred of evidence against Tracey. Only hearsay.'

'Hearsay?'

'That's what it's known as in law,' said Pollock soberly.

With still more desperate hopes dashed Sarah Jane began to twitch again. 'Then Tracey's got to be found,' she said shrilly. 'He's got to be told we're on to him, to be frightened off this wicked, insane thing.'

'Yes, all right,' agreed the Commander. 'But where to find him. It's certain he'll not be back here tonight.'

'He's got to be somewhere. Didn't you say he had a mother?'

'Mother?'

'Yes,' said Sarah Jane a little hysterically, 'perhaps she's one . . . one of the coven. Isn't it supposed to run in families?'

The Commander smiled slightly.

'And I don't think it's funny!' Sarah Jane suddenly shouted and burst into tears. Pollock went to her quickly and put an arm about her heaving shoulders.

'Now, come on, come on,' he said gently. 'You've been wonderful until now. Quite wonderful.'

'Sorry,' sniffed Sarah Jane. 'Sorry.'

'Don't apologise!'

The grieving, angry girl took out a handkerchief and blew her nose violently. 'Right, where does she live?'

'Who?'

'Tracey's mother.'

'In Beaminster.'

'Where's that?'

'About five miles the other side of Halstock.'

Everything came together at once for Sarah Jane. Wilson wasn't going to Halstock, he was going to Beaminster. 'You'll not get to Halstock!' Tracey had shouted, meaning that the policeman wouldn't even get halfway. Forgetting herself completely she hit the Commander excitedly on the arm. 'That's where he is,' she cried, her eyes shining. 'That's where he is. Brendan's with his mother.'

'By George!' said Pollock so infected by her excitement he wasn't conscious of the pun, 'I believe you're right.'

'Of course I'm right. Come on!'

'No, wait,' said the Commander. 'We can't do this alone. There'll be more to deal with besides Tracey and his mother, you can be sure of that. We need help.'

'We've got help,' said Sarah Jane happily. 'We've got all the help we need in K –' She stopped herself in time, quickly debating with herself the wisdom of continued secrecy about the robot. She convinced herself that to reveal K9 at this stage would only take up precious time.

So intent were the two on the implications of Sarah Jane's shrewd deduction that neither saw Tracey appear outside the window and disappear just as quickly. 'What help?' asked Sarah Jane moderately.

'The police, of course.'

'But you've just said . . .'

'This is different,' interrupted Pollock. 'No question of a warrant. Nothing as disrupting as a raid. Just some men front and back and a polite enquiry concerning the whereabouts of George Tracey. Nothing simpler. Come on, let's get out of here. The place is beginning to give me the creeps.' He opened the door and let Sarah Jane and Jasper pass him before switching off the light. 'I'll get on to Jimmie now.'

'Who's Jimmie?'

'Sir James Taylor, Chief Constable,' said the Commander relocking the door. Sarah Jane was already feeling happier. At last something was going to be done. At last those in authority were about to be enlisted.

George Tracey came smoothly out of the dark into the moonlight, watching the plotters on their way back to the Manor.

'It's not too late?' asked Sarah Jane anxiously.

'I ought to be able to get him,' said Pollock. 'Or if not him, Harrison, his deputy.'

'No, I meant to go to Beaminster tonight.'

'Oh, it won't be tonight,' said the Commander. 'It won't happen tonight. I'm sure our police force is up to it logistically. But it is springing it a bit.' Sarah Jane groaned in disappointment. 'Don't you worry, m'dear,' said Pollock reassuringly. 'There'll be no time lost. The boy's going to be all right. First light. That's the time for the short, sharp, shock. That's the time for surprises. That's the time that's least expected. No time to deploy, no time to regroup. Tactics.'

They'd reached the front door of the Manor. 'There,' said the Commander. 'What you need is a good night's rest. Got any pills?'

'No,' said Sarah Jane dully. 'Never take them.'

'Try a good tot of whisky in a mug of hot milk. I'll get on to Jimmie now and give you a ring.'

Sarah Jane was so dispirited that she didn't remember her telephone was still out of order until the Commander's footsteps no longer trod the gravel. She let herself into the hall, desperately wanting to talk to K9, a plan forming quickly in her mind. What if they went to Beaminster together tonight under cover of darkness? By all accounts Tracey had run in terror from K9. Brendan had gone into that in great detail. If Tracey had reacted like that, wouldn't his mother do the same? But where to go? How to get the address?

She dashed into the sitting-room and attacked the telephone directory. There were two Traceys in Beaminster. She would have to go out to a telephone box: taking Pollock into her confidence was out of the question. If Tracey answered she had simply to hang up, home and dry. If his mother answered: may I speak to George? Same again. His mother had a choice of responses. She could hang up or ask who was speaking or say George wasn't there. Home and dry. If whoever answered denied knowledge of someone called George she had only one conclusion to draw. There would be need for but one telephone call, that's all. Simple.

Excited, she ran out to the kitchen to consult K9. As she opened the cupboard the front door bell jangled frighteningly. 'K9,' she whispered.

'Mistress.'

123

'I'm going to open the front door.' She very nearly added, 'Cover me,' but picked up a large, sharp kitchen knife instead. As she crossed the hall K9 positioned himself so that he could hear without being seen and advanced his blaster. Sarah Jane opened the front door with the knife pressed flat against her leg.

'Forgot about your phone,' said Pollock.

'Come in,' said Sarah Jane insincerely.

'No, no! You'll need all the rest you can get. It's on for tomorrow.'

'Oh, good!' she said, 'Oh, good!' flourishing the knife unconsciously.

'I thought you'd like to know. Settle you down a bit. If you want to be there . . .'

'Oh, yes! Yes!'

'If you want to be there, be ready to leave at six. All right?'

'Oh, yes! Thank you, Commander, thank you.'

'A pleasure,' said Pollock gruffly. 'Very wise,' he added.

'Wise?' asked Sarah Jane, puzzled.

'That,' he said, pointing at the knife not two feet from his nose. Sarah Jane looked at the thing in her hand in some surprise, having forgotten its existence. 'Oh,' she said with a mirthless laugh, 'just making myself a sandwich.'

'Good tot of whisky in a mug of hot milk,' he said. 'Good night.' And then he was gone.

Sarah Jane locked and bolted the doors and checked all the windows. 'Come on, K9,' she said, 'beddibyes.' But she didn't open the kitchen cupboard. She led the Doctor's robot upstairs. She knew she wasn't going to sleep a wink.

Within the reach of the light of the moon, within the dancing yellow glow of the four guttering torches, within the mystic confines of the pentacle, within the overgrown ruins in the thicket clearing, the initiation ceremony was nearing its climax. Ten black-shrouded figures ringed Peter Tracey whose cloak was too big for him, being that one which had been worn until recently by the late Vince Wilson.

He stood, resigned to what was happening, terror-stricken at the thought of sharing the policeman's fate and that of his mother five years earlier. He watched the High Priestess turn from the High Priest to face him, the novice. He watched her raise her arms to the moon, the athame in her right hand and the cord in her left. He shuddered at the sound of the voice distorted by the grotesque goat mask.

'I invoke thee and call upon thee, O Mighty Mother of all, bringer of all fruitfulness by seed and root, by stem and bud, by leaf and flower and fruit; by life and love do we invoke thee to descend upon the body of thy servant and priestess that the body and soul of they servant Peter Tracey be offered unto thee.'

The ten cloaked figures began to chant as they slowly circled the initiate to the Hazelbury Abbas coven.

'Hecate, Hecate, Hecate . . .'

12

Halstock

Sarah Jane had slept little and then only in fitful dozes with bad, irrelevant dreams. She'd gone over the old factual ground exhaustively with K9 and, in so doing, had learned something of his surprising versatility. Not only did he incorporate all the capacity of an advanced computer, including scanning and memorising graphic material at photographic speed, but his blaster, with which he could kill or stun, was also capable of adaptation to penetrate matter of any density, of which stone and steel were prime examples. He was also equipped with a small probe which gave him manual dexterity.

She was ready and waiting long before the appointed hour, fidgeting and fretting as time limped heavily by. She drank more coffee than was good for her and ate nothing which was even worse.

At five minutes to six she could bear the waiting no longer. She decided to anticipate the arrival of the police or the Commander or both, expecting the constabulary to call on Pollock first. She left K9 to his own devices, let herself out of the house and hurried to the east wing in torchlight.

Long before she reached the door her stomach churned at the long howls of an unhappy dog that could only be coming from Jasper. Her torch showed the front door to be ajar. She pushed it wide and groped for a light switch, the howling getting to her like a knife. The door to the sitting-room stood open with the lights on beyond. She called out the Commander's name and ran through the open door. The room, normally untidy, was a shambles. She ran back across the hall to the door behind which Jasper was now scratching. As she pushed it open the dog backed away with bared teeth, snarling savagely. He was as afraid of Sarah Jane as she of him. Jasper went back on his haunches, lifted his head and howled heart-rendingly. Sarah Jane closed the door and called again, as despairingly as the dog: 'Commander! Commander Pollock!' She rushed to open all the doors in the annexe, to rooms empty save for furniture shrouded in dust sheets; to cupboards; to the only bedroom in use on the first floor which had not been slept in. Pollock was gone. Gone! And, without a doubt, the victim of foul play. She put her face in her hands and sobbed. The dog's howling drove her to action. She dashed into the sitting-room. It was five minutes past six. Where were the police? She grabbed the handset of the telephone and dialled 999. Inarticulate with extreme anxiety she gave the particulars, her own address, and left. The howling dog was beyond bearing.

She 'kennelled' K9 after telling him of the attack on Pollock. His silence, his acceptance of the information without comment, was even worse to bear than the grieving Jasper. The police were quickly on the spot: two young constables from Sherborne, polite, sympathetic and eager to help. Sarah Jane showed them the annexe and they took charge of Jasper, having to muzzle him first. She felt foolish, lost, desperately alone and tongue-tied. Not knowing what had passed between Pollock and the Chief Constable and not being able to substantiate the claim that the late Sergeant Wilson was a witch there was little she could tell the policemen beyond a rendezvous arranged by the Commander for six o'clock that morning. The two young men were ignorant of any such rendezvous at Sherborne and a call from their car confirmed that the police there were not involved. If the Chief Constable had knowledge of it Dorchester would be the best people to talk to. She asked to be able to speak to Sir James Taylor. They were sorry but that was something that couldn't be arranged by them, but if she would like to have a word with Superintendent Johnson . . .

By this time deep despair had reduced Sarah Jane to the nadir of dismay and self-pity. She looked tearfully at the two fresh-faced boys in blue and could clearly see their reaction to a preposterous statement to the effect that Brendan

Richards, a fourteen-year-old boy in her charge, had been kidnapped by one George Tracey who, together with the late Sergeant Wilson was a member of a witches' coven, and that the said George Tracey intended the said Brendan Richards to be sacrificed at a black magic ceremony, and that the intended human sacrifice was being held prisoner by the said George Tracey's mother in Beaminster. She could see the tight smiles of embarrassment, the averted eyes, the shuffling feet. What was meant by the adage 'truth is stranger than fiction' was, of course, 'truth is less believable than fiction.' People believed what they wanted to believe and that was that.

The policeman left her with assurances that everything that could be done would be done to find George Tracey and Commander Pollock, both of whom enjoyed great respect and popularity within their community. Sarah Jane went into the kitchen, sat at the table and wept.

'Mistress?' The muffled voice of K9 did nothing but increase her misery.

'Go away!' she shouted tearfully. 'Just go away and leave me alone!'

'Mistress?'

'Go away, you horrible little tin . . .!' She couldn't think of a suitable epithet, and he couldn't go away. But she could shut him up, shut him off. She got up and opened the cupboard door violently. 'Right! Out!' she ordered. K9 glided out of his kennel, his tail wagging in gratitude. Or so it seemed to an overwrought Sarah Jane suddenly overcome with shame. 'Oh, K9, I'm so sorry!' she said, 'but I'm in such a state.'

'Suggest Bakers,' crooned K9.

'Suggest Bakers?'

'Bakers,' repeated K9. 'Neighbours,' he reminded her.

The Bakers. Of course! She didn't care for them that much but they were people of influence and did claim to be friends of Aunt Lavinia. 'Thank you, K9,' she said. 'Thank you very much,' and she stooped and kissed him between the ears.

Juno Baker put down her coffee cup, toyed with the piece of

toast on her plate and looked at Sarah Jane across the breakfast table. 'My dear,' she murmured gently, but with a calculated upward inflection, 'human sacrifice?'

Sarah Jane instantly regretted she'd come, regretted she'd poured out the whole presposterous story to the Bakers in a desperate bid for help. In her heart she'd known that this comfortable, middle-class, conservative couple would be unable to accept any statement that threatened to subvert the establishment, that pointed an accusing finger at the police.

'I'm sorry,' she said distantly. 'I shouldn't have come.' As she got up to go Juno put out a hand to detain her.

'No. Don't go, please. Sit down, dear, do. You were perfectly right to come. But Bill will be about somewhere. He won't have disappeared.'

'But he has!' said Sarah Jane loudly, sitting again and slapping the table with the flat of her hand. 'So has Tracey. And what's more their cars are still there, the Range Rover and the Ford Escort. I checked before I came.'

'Have you talked to any of the workers at all?'

'Yes, of course I have. But they don't live in the place and they don't like being asked questions. They make that very plain.'

Howard Baker came back into the dining-room holding a glass which contained a generous measure of brandy. He put it on the table in front of his fraught guest. 'Here, try this.'

Sarah Jane watched him resume his place at the table without looking at her. It was an action that spoke volumes. She looked from husband to wife. 'You don't believe a word I've said, do you?'

'My dear, you're upset,' said Juno soothingly.

'Of course I'm upset!' exploded Sarah Jane. 'The police are politely suggesting I'm nuts and you're humouring me. I didn't imagine all this, you know. I'm *compus mentis and* and experienced journalist.'

'Of course you are,' Howard Baker said. 'But there must be a rational explanation for all this.'

Sarah Jane turned on him indignantly. 'Am I being irrational? First Aunt Lavinia goes off without a word and then Brendan is kidnapped.' She rounded on Juno who had quietly cleared her throat. 'Yes! Kidnapped!'

'The police seem to think,' said Juno unhurriedly, 'that the boy may have climbed down from the window.'

'Oh,' hooted Sarah Jane, 'really!'

'That's what they told Howard.'

'And why?'

'Why what, dear?'

'Why should Brendan climb out of the window?'

'I really don't know,' said Juno equably, 'Who knows what boys that age have got in their heads? Have you checked at the school?'

It was something that Sarah Jane hadn't thought of doing. The thought that the boy might have made his way back to school hadn't occurred to her: there was no reason for it. 'No,' she said.

'Well, then,' said Juno, clearly suggesting that it was an omission that should be given serious thought.

'He couldn't possibly have gone back to school.'

'How can you be so sure?'

Sarah Jane could be so sure because there was nothing at school to compare with the fascination of K9, but because her story had been told without reference to the robot she had to reply unconvincingly. 'Because I am.'

Juno Baker shrugged and went back to her piece of toast. Sarah Jane looked from one to the other of them. 'All right, how do you explain Commander Pollock arranging to meet me at six o'clock this morning and then wrecking his sitting-room, shutting up his dog and going off without his Range Rover?' Husband and wife exchanged a look, a look which was intercepted by Sarah Jane.

'I think you should know,' said Howard evenly, 'that Bill Pollock has quite a reputation locally as a bit of an eccentric.'

'Really,' said Sarah Jane, not without sarcasm. 'Well, eccentric or not, he never goes anywhere without that dog of his.'

'I've just been on the telephone,' said Howard quietly, spooning out the bottom of his egg. 'Sergeant Wilson died of a heart attack last night.'

'Am I saying he didn't,' snapped Sarah Jane.

'Sarah, dear,' said Juno softly. 'Why don't you . . .?' She indicated the brandy glass with a delicate finger.

'Thank you, but eight o'clock in the morning is just a shade early even for a deranged *rouée* like me.'

Juno Baker withdrew slightly, exchanging another look with her husband. Sarah Jane was contrite. They were both doing their best to be of some small comfort to her and it wasn't exactly their fault that she wasn't getting through. 'I'm sorry,' she said, 'that was discourteous of me.'

'More coffee?'

'No, thanks. I think it's high time I went. Thanks for listening.'

'No, my dear,' said Howard Baker, 'don't go like that.'

'Change your mind,' invited Juno offering the pot.

'All right. Thanks.'

Juno dispensed the coffee. 'My dear . . .' – her tone couldn't have been more dulcet – '. . . witches . . . black magic . . . human sacrifice . . . it's all very romantic, but this *is* 1981.'

'Aunt Lavinia found evidence of a revival at least,' countered Sarah Jane.

'She found relics,' agreed Juno.

'Which are found regularly all over the country,' added Howard.

'She made me a present of one,' said Juno. 'You saw it when you were here last.'

'Oh?'

'The athame. The ceremonial knife. On the wall.'

Sarah Jane remembered the thing peered at by the revolting Henry Tobias. 'Oh, yes.' She took a sip of her coffee, put down the cup and said steadily. 'If you disbelieve everything I've told you, it's tantamount to calling me a liar.'

'Not at all,' said Howard smoothly. 'Let me ask you something. Where were you when you overheard Tracey and Wilson? Where exactly?' Again Sarah Jane was being kicked in her Achilles heel. Unerringly on the same sore spot. But of one thing she was absolutely certain. Any reference to K9 at this stage wouldn't only wreck her credibility: they'd be ringing up for an ambulance to take her away. 'Just outside the Tracey cottage,' she said.

'They were how far away from you?'

'They were inside,' admitted Sarah Jane with misgiving.

'Ah,' pounced Howard, 'then isn't it possible that you might have misheard part of what they had to say?'

'No, it's *not* possible,' said Sarah Jane, fully conscious that it was the most irrational statement she'd made in her entire life. She remained unsurprised as husband and wife exchanged yet another meaningful look, and looked straight ahead as Juno rose from her chair and came to sit next to her to put a comforting arm about her shoulders.

'Darling child, why don't you go home and put your feet up?' she suggested warmly. 'I'll ring Doctor Perry and ask him to drop in. Howard'll find Bill for you. And he'll get your telephone fixed. He's not without some pull round here.'

It was at that very moment that Sarah Jane remembered when and where she'd first heard of Halstock. Pollock had spoken of it on her arrival. The Bakers farmed there, he'd said. With a bigger place there than they had here. Numb with shock and with her skin crawling at the weight of Juno Baker's arm on her shoulders she got up quickly and said, 'Yes, I'll do that. Thank you.'

K9 was in the sitting-room immersed in the library on witchcraft. It surrounded him in methodical piles on the floor; books, pamphlets, manuscripts, notes. As he heard the front door open and positioned himself defensively behind the sofa. Sarah Jane closed the front door and made straight for the kitchen expecting K9 to be where she'd left him.

She called out K9's name but the robot remained hidden in the event that Mistress was not alone. She was impulsive and that led to carelessness. The order was that his existence should remain a secret.

Sarah Jane came breathlessly into the room. 'K9?' she said. The robot waited long enough to assess with accuracy that his owner was unaccompanied and then glided out from behind the sofa. Sarah Jane, thankful for K9's diligence, had to bite back the 'good dog' that came unbidden to her lips. She stooped to squint at what seemed to occupy the robot's interest and then levered herself onto the sofa. 'Listen, K9,' she said excitedly. 'You were right about the Bakers. How did you know?'

'Mistress?'

'Oh, come on, K9, that the Bakers have Brendan.'

'Ignorant of such knowledge, Mistress.'

'What? But it was you that pointed to them.'

'As neighbours, Mistress.'

'Neighbours?'

'In the human condition a neighbour alleviates distress,' droned K9.

'Oh! Well, they've got Brendan, I'm sure of it. I've been putting two and two together.'

'Two and two do not always make four.'

'What?'

'Mathematical anomaly,' pointed out K9.

Here we go again, thought Sarah Jane. 'Never mind all that,' she said impatiently. 'The snag is that there's no evidence. But it's obvious Tracey's in with them. They're all witches.'

'No evidence against Tracey,' reminded K9.

'I know, I know,' said Sarah Jane with a trace of irritation, 'but I'm convinced Brendan's at Halstock after all. The Bakers have a farm there and you should have heard them this morning.' K9 was silent. 'Well, what are we going to do?'

'Is conviction based on evidence?'

'No, but that doesn't prevent us going there, does it?'

'Affirmative.'

Sarah Jane wrinkled her nose and pursed her lips looking at K9 with something akin to dislike. He was right. He was *always* right. She slumped back on the sofa. Perhaps hell was like this; telling the truth to people who couldn't believe you. The diabolical thing about it was that she could see both sides. If she were asked to believe that Howard and Juno Baker were witches . . . could she? Capable of sacrificing a fourteen-year-old boy . . . could she? And yet she knew it for a fact that they were, for all K9's reminder that she had no evidence. 'All right, K9, what's to stop me looking round that farm at Halstock?'

'Nothing,' agreed K9.

'That's what I'll do then,' said Sarah Jane, sitting up.

'If assumption correct Brendan at farm those responsible for abduction aware of Mistress knowledge.'

'Meaning I haven't got a hope of finding him there?'

'Affirmative.'

She knew he was right again. She was up against lack of evidence, the law of trespass, social privilege, political influence and the indigenous population closing ranks. A formidable array.

She sagged into the sofa again. Nervous exhaustion and lack of sleep combined in a sort of torpor and she entered that semiconscious state of the borders of sleep. Half-formed images floated behind closed eyelids; amorphous shapes reflecting the harrowing experiences of the last few days. The shapes took form and became focused. She saw prancing cloaked forms, grotesque in firelight, performing barbaric rites. She saw witches, warlocks, goblins, demons. She came awake. That was it! The last hope, but a good one. The enemy had to come into the open to function. From what little she'd read on the subject the elements could only be invoked when the coven was exposed to them, and in exposing itself to the elements it exposed itself to other forces – the forces of law and order. That was it! That was the answer! With the return of hope came renewed excitement. She sat up. 'K9?'

'Mistress?'

She pointed to the books and papers on the floor. 'Is there anything in that lot to tell us where Aunt Lavinia may have found relics?'

'Negative.'

'Listen, K9, we've got to find out where this coven performs its ceremonies. It's got to be somewhere local. Now, if we can do that there's a good chance we could put a stop to them. With any luck we could even catch them in the act. What about that?'

'Able to serve Mistress,' was K9's ready response. 'Require large scale map of area.'

'Right,' agreed Sarah Jane, coming to her feet like a spring and rapidly searching the bookshelves. 'Ordnance Survey. There are some here. I've seen them. Yes!' She'd found a number of the maps grouped together. She chose number 194 and opened it to spread it on the floor in front of K9 who had begun to offer a précis of his researches. 'Data witchcraft in England. Primitive traditional belief in rural areas cosmic forces control weather to secure crops. Occult ceremonies invoke such forces. Most important ceremony falls on winter solstice: December twenty-second.'

'That's tomorrow!'

'Affirmative.'

Sarah Jane eagerly watched K9 who began methodically to scan the map. 'What are you looking for?' she asked.

'Witches power increased by hallowed ground.'

'Churches!'

'Affirmative.'

'Oh, K9, how clever!'

'What signifies a church?'

Sarah Jane unfolded the legend tucked under the side of the map saying: 'A black oblong or ball with a cross on top.'

'Within what radius?' asked K9.

Sarah Jane thought for a moment. 'Say five miles.'

'There are eleven,' responded K9 instantly. Sarah Jane crouched close to the robot, studying the map and K9 pointed to the area under review with his probe. 'Circumference of circle from here to here.'

'East Coker to Batcombe,' murmured Sarah Jane. 'That covers an awful lot of ground. There must be a way of narrowing it down.'

'Ruins,' said K9 without hesitation.

'Ruins?'

'Logical assumption,' resumed K9, 'clandestine activity sequestered.'

'So?' asked Sarah Jane puzzled.

'Hallowed ground never deconsecrated except by government order *ergo* hallowed ground disused.'

'Ruined churches!'

'Or ruins near rebuilt churches.'

'Oh, you are clever, K9.'

'Affirmative.'

Sarah Jane's face clouded a little. She quickly traced a finger over the selected area. 'The snag is that it doesn't narrow it down at all. Ruins aren't always marked on these maps. I'm afraid there's nothing for it but to look at the lot. Can you work out the quickest route to look at all of them?'

Affirmative.'

'Then let's go as soon as possible. You can get into the holdall and I'll put you in the car. We've got until tomorrow night.'

'Negative, Mistress. Winter solstice December twenty-second begins after midnight tonight.'

Sarah Jane was rocked. Of course! Most people got so used to sleeping through the beginning of every day their sense of time was automatically pushed forward. She jumped with shock at the sudden shrilling of the telephone, recovered, and rushed to answer it. 'Yes?' she gasped.

Juno Baker's soft voice purred into her ear. 'There, dear, you've got your telephone back.' Howard Baker certainly had got pull. 'Just thought I'd check. How are you feeling?'

Sarah Jane was thankful for the distance between them. It allowed her to dissemble without the difficulty of being face to face with a woman she knew to be the personification of evil. 'A little better, thank you.'

'Oh, good! Listen, my dear, I've been talking to Howard. We don't think you should be on your own. Why don't you come over to dinner?'

'Tonight?' said Sarah Jane, conscious of the silliness of the question but already alert to the implications of the invitation.

'Yes,' went on Juno vibrantly. 'It'll take your mind off things. And by then we might have some news for you. Who knows?'

I know, thought Sarah Jane. She said, 'It's very kind of you but I am a little tired.'

'Oh, we won't be late. We'll have you tucked up in bed long before midnight.'

So that was it. Make sure the girl was tucked neatly away. As neatly as Bill Pollock had been disposed of. Neater. In her case there would be no need of violence. 'It's more than kind of you but I'd be very poor company.'

'All right, my dear.' Sarah Jane could hear the disappointment in the dulcet voice. 'But if you should change your mind we'll be delighted to see you. Give us a ring and we'll come and get you. You'll be able to tipple to your heart's content.'

And to yours, thought Sarah Jane. She thanked Juno and hung up. The Bakers were going to have to think of something else, weren't they?'

'K9, I'm right,' she said triumphantly.

K9 was silent. Cheeky thing, thought Sarah Jane almost happily.

13

Evil Under the Moon

It was nearly midday before a fretful Sarah Jane was ready to leave. She had received a number of telephone calls all of which had been unimportant save for one: Reuters reporting from New York an inability to track down Doctor Lavinia Smith. PC Carter from West Norton had called for what seemed to be an unnecessary duplication of her statement to the Sherborne police concerning the last known movements of George Tracey and Commander Pollock.

She'd brought the MGB round from the garage and succeeded in getting the heavy holdall into the car unseen. K9 was ensconced on the floor at the back equipped with the Ordnance Survey map and an ordered list of the hallowed ground to be scrutinised. After a discussion on tactics with K9, of which Commander Pollock would have heartily approved, Sarah Jane had decided to deliver a copy of their itinerary to the Sherborne police in the hope that one, they would see reason, and two, her intention would percolate to members of the coven by way of the local bush telegraph.

She entered Sherborne from the A352 turning right along Westbury after crossing the River Yeo. In Digby Road, no more than a hundred yards from the police station, she saw the white TR7 for the first time. It was illegally parked. All right for some, she thought. She pulled up near the garage opposite the squat modern police station in one with the Magistrates Court and looked round at the blanketed robot.

'All right, K9?'

'Affirmative.'

'But keep your voice down.'

'Affirmative,' obeyed a muted K9. Sarah Jane opened the door of the car and then closed it with a snap. Coming out of the police station was none other than Howard Baker. Her first thought was to hide but then she realised that here was a splendid opportunity to aim at two birds with a single stone. If she told Howard Baker of her plan she would have no need of the bush telegraph. She tooted her horn and waved happily. Howard Baker acknowledged the signal with a wide smile and came hurrying towards her. 'Why, hello again,' he said.

'Thanks for fixing the telephone.'

'Oh, Juno rang you. Good. A severed cable,' he explained.

'A severed cable,' echoed Sarah Jane derisively.

'Yes,' grinned Howard, 'a bit twee, isn't it? The engineer's words, not mine. You've come in to see the police?'

'That's right. I've come to let them have a copy of my plan.'

'Your plan?'

'My plan. I'm going to take a good look round suitable stamping grounds for a witches' coven. I've got quite an impressive list. Drawn up by a computer from considerable data,' she added mischievously. She watched the man's face closely. The smile relaxed a little but he answered cheerfully enough.

'Well, that'll keep you busy.' The minimal reaction was no disappointment to Sarah Jane. She'd never ceased to wonder at the evil that could be masked by a handsome face. 'Shall we see you tonight?'

'It's sweet of you. I asked Juno if I might think about it.'

'Oh, do come. If you give me a ring I can collect you.'

'And get me drunk.'

The wide smile returned. 'I can't promise you that but be sure you're more than welcome.'

'Oh, I am sure. Thank you.'

'Till later then.' And with his smile wider than ever Howard Baker walked leisurely away to where his Rolls Bentley was also illegally parked. Oh, yes, he had pull all right. Sarah Jane watched him drive off and promptly parked the MGB in the vacated space. She'd see how much pull she had; a citizen of the realm who to date had made two serious complaints without any satisfaction. She collected her bag from the passenger seat, crossed the road and walked up a long ramp to the double doors which she pushed open. The counter was directly in front of her. It was a busier place than West Norton although there seemed to be little uniformed activity. The sergeant on duty had a trim if slightly faded military look and was busy sifting through a file of paper. Sarah Jane opened her bag, produced her list and placed it before the unsurprised officer of the law. 'Have a look at that while you're about it,' she said.

Sergeant Matthews picked up the list and gave it a cursory glance which betrayed a total lack of concern. 'What's this?' he asked.

'A list.'

'It does look rather like one, yes.' He fixed Sarah Jane with a look which clearly said, 'and I want no cheek from you, my girl.'

'I'd better introduce myself.'

'That might be helpful, Miss,' said Matthews drily.

'I'm Sarah Jane Smith from Bradleigh Manor, Hazelbury Abbas.'

The Sergeant's neutral expression took on a wary look. 'I was in touch with you early this morning.' The policeman clearly remembered. 'About the kidnapping of Commander Pollock.'

'Kidnapping?' The wariness gave way to speculation that this woman could be a nutter. She was a bit on the young side but the report brought back by Worth and Chadwick hadn't been very encouraging.

'That's what I said.'

'I see, miss. And the significance of the list? You think the Commander might be at one of these places?'

'No.'

'Oh.'

'That list is of hallowed ground within a radius of five miles from Hazelbury Abbas.'

'Is that so, now? Interesting.'

'No, it isn't and there's no need to be polite.'

'It's standing order, Miss.'

'That list is of no interest to you but of great interest to me,' went on Sarah Jane inexorably. 'I intend to go to all those places in an attempt to find the ritual ground of a coven of witches who have kidnapped Brendan Richards and intend him to be a human sacrifice.'

'I see,' said Sergeant Matthews with a fixed expression of total composure. 'And you'd like us to . . .' He left the question in the air since it was the best place for it.

'I'd like you to know this in case something happens to me.'

'And what do you think might happen to you?' asked the Sergeant gently, chalking up hysteria and incipient paranoia in about equal proportions.

'There are a number of people who want to stop me.'

'Oh, yes.' This was, sadly, a very large slice of fruit cake. 'Yes, I see,' said Matthews with a monumental calm. 'You wouldn't like to come in and have a cup of tea and go into all this in a little more detail?'

'No, I wouldn't, thank you very much,' said Sarah Jane in high disdain. 'And stop humouring me! I'm not mad.'

Sergeant Matthews watched the girl dispassionately as she flounced out and reached for the telephone.

'They think I'm mad,' said Sarah Jane flopping into the driving seat. 'Frankly, I didn't expect anything else.'

'Mistress?'

'The police think I'm insane – and keep your voice down!'

'Conflict between good and evil,' droned K9 quietly, 'in concept of human moral values the root of insanity.'

'That's their excuse, is it?' said Sarah Jane tartly. 'Yes, all right, K9, that's quite enough of that, thank you. Let's get on with it, shall we?' She rummaged in her bag for her copy of the list and half-smiled at the name that headed it. 'We can elbow the first one,' she said.

'Elbow, Mistress?'

'Sorry, K9. To erase, to forget about. East Coker's where T. S. Eliot is buried.'

'T. S. Eliot?'

'A great poet and a man of the Church. No witch would dare to go near there, I'm sure. Right, that makes Trent the first on the list.'

'A30 going west right turn signpost Over Compton five miles,' said K9 briskly.

'Great stuff, K9!' enthused Sarah Jane warmly, 'Keep it coming like that!'

Trent was little more than a hamlet, modern stone-built dwellings nestling with the old. The church was tucked back from the winding road behind walls of uneven height. Sarah Jane parked the MGB by a triangle of grass where the road broadened at the entrance and walked through the tall, wrought iron gates that were standing open. She came upon the rectory so suddenly it might have been put there at that moment for her benefit. She looked at the sunken fifteenth-century building, with its tiny mullioned windows staring back at her like sightless eyes, and trembled with both excitement and fear. It was only then that she remembered seeing nobody in the village from the time she entered it. Not a sign. Not a soul. Could this be what she was looking for? There could very well be ruins here. The first on her list? Luck? Or had fate led her here?

She moved towards the church, its sharp spire thrusting from between four short pinnacles like an inert fabulous beast watching for prey. As she drew nearer, the worn, lichen-covered gargoyles took on ugly, sinister shapes. This had got to be the place. Then she took sudden notice of the pedestal-like memorial to her left, the new white stone shining from amongst the ancient, lurching tombstones. Disappointment hit her as unexpectedly as a slap in the face. Carved in a flat stone level with the surrounding grass was the inscription: *Geoffrey Francis Fisher ninety-ninth Archbishop of Canterbury and Rosamund his wife.*

The sight transformed the place, pushing back distorted images, sinister shapes, dark thoughts. No coven could flourish its evil here. She saw the church and the yard anew with shining eyes, finding it hard to believe that human beings could be depraved enough to desecrate the beauty of such a place, to parody the simple worship that brought comfort and peace to the unquiet heart. She went into the church and prayed.

The second church on the revised list was at Sutton Bingham through which Sarah Jane remembered passing the night before on the way to Halstock. Saying nothing to K9 she resolved to take a look at the Baker farm en route. Sutton Bingham, she decided, was too near East Coker and the remains of Thomas Stearns Eliot to be worth more than a cursory look and she was anxious to get on to the farm. Their next call was at Fromisham and K9 had confirmed they had to by-pass Halstock to get there.

She saw the white TR7 again as she put her foot down on the straight stretch of road running along the west bank of the reservoir. It suddenly appeared in the rear mirror and looked to be closing on her fast. She expected it to pass her but the white sports car remained close behind her, declining to overtake but creeping closer and closer to her. If Sarah Jane hated timidity and indecision on the road she hated even more drivers who didn't keep at a safe distance. Her frayed nerves drove her foot down on the throttle although she was well aware that the increase in speed was a dangerous approach to the bends in the road she knew lay ahead. The TR7 also increased speed and very soon was as close behind her as before but still declining to overtake.

Sarah Jane began to get angry. What was the fool trying to do? She studied the idiot in the rear mirror. It looked to be a young man wearing a cloth cap and a wool scarf that effectively hid any identifiable features. Her long look in the mirror nearly resulted in her coming to grief at a sharp bend. She adjusted her speed by changing down rather than using the footbrake, hoping her unsignalled reduction in speed might shock the chump into backing off. It had the reverse effect. The slackened speed closed the gap between the two cars but the driver of the TR7 came even closer.

Sarah Jane decided that a direct enquiry, couched in no uncertain terms, concerning the imbecile's mental health could do less harm than a bump in her rear. She signalled a slow down and stopped. The TR7 immediately overtook and sped ahead. All right, she thought, get lost! But the car ahead distanced itself only four hundred yards before it, too, came to a stop.

Right, if that's the way you want it, thought Sarah Jane, and went into gear, changing up quickly, to roar past the white sports car which instantly gave chase. But again there was no overtaking. It came up close to the MGB's tail and stayed there. Sarah Jane fumed. The fool was fancying his chances. She'd met the type often. They saw a girl in a sports car and set about showing off. Well, she'd show *him*! 'Route, K9?'

'Left at Halstock right at T junction.'

It was going to take her away from the farm but she'd double back. Nearing Halstock she gained on a tractor, with the TR7 still hugging her tail, and smiled tightly to herself. She stayed behind the tractor but held back from it far enough to see what lay ahead of it. Within sight of the signposted left turn she glanced in her rear mirror at the car behind without turning her head, not wanting to telegraph her next move. Judging the speed of the tractor and the distance she had to cover perfectly, she overtook the tractor and cut in front of it with only a foot or two to spare to make the left turn. A blast from the tractor's horn communicated its driver's extreme disapproval of the manoeuvre. 'Sorry, tractor,' grinned Sarah Jane seeing, with satisfaction, that the TR7 was still behind the tractor as both vehicles moved out of her mirror.

Her joy was shortlived. The white sports car reappeared in the mirror closing fast. This time, instead of staying close behind her, it overtook, drew level and held that position before edging slowly nearer to her off side. Sarah Jane was forced to get away by steering dangerously near the ditch fringed by a barrier of trees. Then she saw something that caused an uncomfortable prickling in the nape of her neck, and made the palms of her hands sweat. The driver of the perilously close car wasn't behaving according to type. He wasn't grinning with self-love, waving cheerily or even blowing a kiss. He was looking directly ahead; directly ahead but with an eye for the narrowing gap between the two cars. This character was trying to drive her off the road and not for the fun of it. He was going to wreck her, to kill her. And his earlier, systematic harrassment was to set her up; to terrorise her into doing something foolish and so contribute to a fatal accident. He was one of *them*. She braked sharply to a sickening squeal and a pungent smell of rubber. The TR7 shot on ahead for a hundred yards and stopped.

Sarah Jane's heart pounded violently and her chest hurt. She watched the man in the car ahead for any sign of movement. There was none. He remained menacingly still. If he got out of the car and came towards her she wouldn't hesitate to run at him and if he didn't get out of her path that would be just too bad. But the man might have been asleep for all the movement he made. She knew it might be dangerous to leave her car but she was, after all, a karate black belt and she doubted her opponent would be. She doubted also that he would be armed. She also knew that if she drove past him he would be in immediate pursuit. She made up her mind that if he wasn't coming to her then she would go to him. She got out of the car and began to walk. The man moved. He went into gear and drove off to come to another halt two hundred yards further on. She stopped. The pattern was quite clear. He wanted her back in the car. He'd no intention of facing her when he killed her. He wanted her in a mangled wreck. She was surprised to realise that her heart had stopped banging away for dear life. Knowing exactly where she stood had a calming affect on her.

She walked back to her car and got into the driving seat, her head quite clear. There were two things she could do. She could wait for a passing car and seek help or she could take her would-be assassin on at his own game. It never occurred to her to enlist K9's physical help but she hadn't forgotten she had his aid. She wanted a look at the road map in order to become familiar with the terrain she would have to tackle ahead but she didn't want the villain, whom she knew would be watching her closely, to read her intention. 'K9?'

'Mistress?'

'What's the layout of the roads ahead? I want right turns, left turns, crossroads, T-junctions, the lot. I want to be able to give someone the slip.'

'Slip, Mistress?'

Sarah Jane smiled grimly. 'I want, K9, to avoid pursuit

and harrassment from a fellow motorist by outwitting him in the manoeuvring of a motor vehicle. Got it?'

'Got it,' said K9 demurely.

'Good, then give!'

'Crossroad ahead. Right turn road ends one mile. Left turn to Evershot. Road beyond crossroad ends T-junction. Left turn road end T-junction with Evershot road. Right turn continues . . .'

'Hang about, hang about!' interrupted Sarah Jane. 'That last left turn sounds as if it completes a triangle.'

'Affirmative. Triangle of approximately equal sides.'

'And the length of a side?'

'One half mile.'

'Thanks, K9. Couldn't be better. Get yourself nicely wedged in there. We're going for a joyride.'

Sarah Jane moved the MGB forward in second gear, coming to a halt four car lengths behind the TR7. 'Make a note of this registration K9! TGX 359F. It's bound to be false but it could help if anything happens to me.' And with that she banged down her foot in second gear and growled past the TR7. Going through into top gear fast she kept to the centre of the road to prevent overtaking. He could ram her in the back is he liked but it was his car against hers. She went over the crossroads and soon saw the T-junction ahead. With the white sports car a short distance behind she turned left into the second side of the triangle and headed for the T-junction with the Evershot road. She turned left again along the final side of the triangle and then repeated the process. She'd completed the course three times, thinking gleefully of the mystification she was provoking behind her, before she saw what she wanted. It was better than she'd hoped for. At the T-junction with Evershot road she saw a line of four cars led by an ancient Renault with an even more ancient driver. The four cars were bunched together and moving at a sedate thirty-five miles an hour. She waited tensely, judging distances, and then shot into the left turn in front of the Renault, giving the TR7 no time or room to make the same manoeuvre and sped away back towards the Halstock Road seeking to get far enough to be out of sight of the TR7 when it had managed to leave behind the caravan of cars still blocking pursuit.

At the crossroads Sarah Jane made the deliberate mistake she hoped would fox the man intent on killing her. She drove straight on up the hill towards West Chelborough, marked as a dead end. She drove on for a mile, reversed the car at a lay-by and waited. The duel had badly eroded her time. She was going to have to abandon her look at the Halstock farm if she was to complete the itinerary. She waited a quarter of an hour to make quite sure her ruse had worked and then drove back the way she'd come. 'We've done it, K9,' she chortled, 'we've done it!'

She'd spoken too soon.

Coming up the hill towards them was the white TR7. Sarah Jane muttered a curse. The man was clever, but not all that clever. She'd fooled him for part of the time, at least. It was evident that he knew the area well and had doubled and redoubled back along the route they'd taken to guess her subterfuge. She had to think quickly. There was no going back. That way there was nowhere to go. She decided to gamble. She had the tactical advantages of position and speed since he was coming up hill. She gunned the stout MGB forward and positioned herself for a head-on collision. Her gamble was that the average male chauvinist pig, behind the wheel of a car, not only treated women drivers with contumely but was firmly of the opinion that, driving without due care and attention, women had charmed lives. She put her foot down hard and steered straight at the TR7. Her gamble paid off. When thirty yards separated the two cars the TR7 swerved violently to its left, went out of control and climbed four feet up the bank at the side of the road before turning turtle, the near side front wheel crushed by the crumpled wing. So much for the car, thought Sarah Jane. She stopped and reversed. The creature deserved all he'd got but common humanity demanded she give what aid was necessary. She was delighted to see there was none needed. Her would-be murderer was crawling from underneath the wreck. She watched him regain his feet without apparent serious effort and then begin a lurching run towards her. She let him come within ten yards; a wild-eyed, wide-mouthed young rat bent on retaliation. Then she slid into gear and moved smoothly away giving him a cheery wave. 'Why don't you take a couple of driving lessons?' she called.

The rear mirror told her her adversary had little more than his pride hurt if she discounted the wreck of his car. The clock on the dashboard told her it was three o'clock. It would be dark in an hour and there remained eight villages to be visited. The loss of daylight would make proper assessment difficult and slow her down but she'd no alternative but to continue with her search.

She drove steadily to Fromisham, aware that anxiety provoked panic and that panic clouded judgement. She knew that if she kept calm, kept control of herself, she would recognise what she was looking for as soon as she saw it. it had to be like that. Fromisham wasn't that place. It was too open, too exposed to give proper cover to what was essentially a clandestine ritual. After the routine consultation with K9 she drove on to Wigworth in rapidly fading light.

In the hay barn it was already dark. Brendan lay unbound and unconscious, comfortably and carefully blanketed. His captors, although outside the law, didn't consider themselves barbarians. The door creaked open and torchlight revealed the visitors as the hirsute Byron Weekes and Michael Barnett, the male nurse.

'He's not moved,' said Weekes.

'He won't,' commented Barnett, 'but I'll look in again later to make sure. It's as it should be. He'll not know a thing about it.' He looked down sadly at the sleeping boy. 'He is graced, blessed to be called unto Hecate.' Byron Weekes lifted melancholy eyes and said:

There is no Grace,
There is no guilt.
This is the law;
Do what thou wilt.

'Something of yours?' asked Barnett.

'Oh, no, no,' murmured the poet modestly. 'It's attributable to Aleister Crowley, but it's more likely to be W. B. Yeats. They were both members of The Golden Dawn in Paris.'

148

Sarah Jane sat in the stationary MGB with the engine running to keep the heater active. It was cold out there in the defiant dark. She looked at the clock. It was already seven-fifteen. Wigworth, Over Hackett and Lillburton explored in the dark with close questioning of the inhabitants had yielded nothing, frustratingly and frighteningly. 'All right, K9,' she sighed, 'what's next?'

'Chiddleholme,' chanted K9. He went on to give precise directions and Sarah Jane moved the car off into the darkness of dwindling hope. There were four more villages to see. It had to be one of these. It had got to be. In five hours the winter solstice would have begun. By her reckoning, calculating the pace of the quest until now, she could cover the ground with only little time to spare. A mile beyond Holnest at Boys Hill the rear offside tyre blew. Unnerved by the loud and unexpected report Sarah Jane wrestled with the wheel to bring the wildly waltzing car under control. It was all she needed. She groped for her torch. 'Know anything about changing wheels, K9?'

'Wheels, Mistress? Please be specific.'

'Motor car wheels.'

'Negative,' said K9 and Sarah Jane together. She opened the boot to get the spare. As she bounced it on the road her stomach muscles knotted. Instead of bounding back the spare was inert and flaccid – flat. She fumbled about for the foot pump praying that the airless tyre was because of her neglect and not the result of something more sinister. Garages in the area were few and far between and she was facing the terrifying prospect of being stranded. She worked away with her foot almost weeping with relief as she began to feel progressive resistance from the tyre. She loosened the wheel nuts and jacked up the car reflecting that K9 did have limitations after all. It was as she was removing the lacerated tyre that the torch played on two even highlights near the jagged wound in the rubber. She leaned the wheel nearer the torch to discover, with a mounting horror, two large brass thumb tacks embedded in the tyre. The blow-out had been no accident. There had been a third tack or even a fourth working away insidiously for how long, she wondered. Her

149

flesh crawled and the sudden sweat on her forehead chilled instantly in the night air. She left the tacks in the tyre. The police would attribute them to an irresponsible childish prank. She knew better.

It was after nine when she reached Chiddleholme and the reconnaissance in the area of the church and the much practised routine enquiry of a nearby cottager corroborated Sarah Jane's initial impression of the place, that it was not what she sought. She returned to the car desperately fighting a clammy, constricting depression. Perhaps this exploration was an enormous mistake. Perhaps the coven pracitised its rites well out of the Hazelbury Abbas area. Howard Baker had listened to her plan with complete equanimity. Had he been laughing at her up his sleeve? Was he, even now, making preparations somewhere the other side of Dorchester? No, that couldn't be. According to Lily Gregson the people upset by Aunt Lavinia were indigenous so the relics must have been found in the area. She had three more villages to call at and less than three hours to do so. Time was running out for her, but far more seriously for Brendan.

Rosemary Creach, the midwife, rose to her feet beside the unconscious boy and stood back to admire her handiwork. She had stripped Brendan of his clothes, annointed his body, and arrayed him in a magnificent cermonial robe that reached from his neck to his feet. His face had been touched here and there with rouge to relieve his pallor and he had been manicured and pedicured.

Rosemary Creach nodded seriously, well pleased with her ministry. She looked towards the door as it groaned open to admit George Lacey and Henry Tobias carrying a long, hazel wood hurdle. The ritual stretcher was set down and the two men carefully and reverently lifted the human sacrifice onto it.

It was a few minutes after eleven when Sarah Jane drove into the last village on the list, Sydling St Nicholas. She knew instantly that her quest had failed but was as determined as she had been in Gossborough and Batcombe to play the cards fate had dealt her to the last. She got out of the car and looked about dispiritedly. Most of the houses and cottages were in darkness but light spilled from the pub warmly and invitingly. The accumulated cigarette smoke in the lounge bar caused her to choke a bit and her eyes to smart but the warmth beckoned. The drinkers-up were few: elderly men perched on bar stools or lurking in secluded corners. The professionally round man behind the bar said, 'I'm afraid you're just too late for a drink, Miss.' Adding instantly, as he took in her pretty, tired and unhappy face, 'I don't know, though. Isn't that clock a bit on the fast side, Bob?'

'It always is,' replied a venerable soul consolidating his precarious perch.

'Thanks,' said Sarah Jane wearily. 'I don't want a drink, but I'd be grateful for an answer to a couple of questions.'

'Sure,' obliged the landlord.

'Are there any ruins round here?'

'There's me,' suggested Bob, shaking on his stool.

'Apart from him,' said Mine Host, 'what sort of ruins?'

'Well, ecclesiastical sort of. A church, an abbey, a convent. Something like that.'

The landlord shook his head. 'Nothing like that around here to my knowledge. Any of you lot know any?'

There was a muttered chorus of assorted negatives out of which rose a tactful question from the venerable Bob. 'Bit late to be looking for that sort of thing, isn't it?'

'Yes, I suppose it is,' agreed Sarah Jane lamely, 'but I'm doing a survey, you see, and I'm a bit pushed for time.'

'Sorry,' said the publican with genuine regret.

'Thanks anyway,' she said automatically. 'Good night.'

The chorus of 'good nights' gave way to a speculative silence as Sarah Jane left the bar. She knew very well what the closing-time topic of conversation would be. When she got back to the car she wasn't conscious of the faint light coming from behind the seats. She sank down behind the wheel and wept bitterly.

'Mistress?'

151

'Oh, shut up, K9,' she said through her tears.

K9 persisted: 'Significance of simple cross?'

'What?' Couldn't the stupid dog see she was upset?

'On the map. Significance of simple cross.'

'Look at the legend!'

'I study the legend, Mistress. What is a chapel?'

'A sort of church,' said Sarah Jane listlessly.

'Please be specific.'

'A private church. One with no parish.'

'There is a ruined chapel at the Manor,' announced K9.

'What Manor?'

'Bradleigh Manor.'

'*What!*' Sarah Jane span round towards K9. Under their very noses? She couldn't believe it! 'Let me see!' She pushed her arm between the seats to take hold of the map and spread it on her knees. She snapped on her torch to pin-point Hazelbury Abbas.

'Follow the footpath to the river,' instructed K9.

'What footpath?'

'To the east of the Manor. Follow it for one quarter of a mile.'

Sarah Jane had never been a good map reader and was too excited to find the Manor let alone the footpath. A ruined chapel a quarter of a mile from the Manor in the middle of farming land. Not overlooked. Secluded. That's *where* Aunt Lavinia found the relics. 'You follow it, K9!' she cried and thrust the map back to him. She looked at the clock. Twenty minutes past eleven. 'How far away are we?' K9 had already made the calculation. 'Fifteen miles.' Fifteen miles in forty minutes, thought Sarah Jane. A piece of cake. 'Route?'

'East to Cerne Abbas. Left on A352 to Holnest.'

The MGB roared off into the night, stirring sleeping heads in the peaceful village of Sydling St Nicholas and provoking an epithet from the lips of the venerable Bob as he tottered happily from the public house.

By the light of the moon thirteen shadows, two bearing the precious hurdle, moved slowly in reverential single file along the footpath to the east of Bradleigh Manor following it

152

towards the river.

Sarah Jane had abandoned all concern for the speed limit on the A352 heading north until she was forced to slow down by a heavy goods vehicle just past Minterne Magna. Try as she may, she couldn't get beyond the monster grinding on inclines and round never-ending bends at a snail-like twenty miles an hour. Every opportunity to overtake was frustrated by the sudden glare of an oncoming car inspiring in Sarah Jane a stream of raving invective which was systematically stored by K9 as relevant to the behaviour of *homo sapiens* under extreme stress. After the fifth aborted attempt to overtake and a glance at the clock which showed thirty-five minutes past eleven Sarah Jane could take no more. 'Alternative route!' she screamed to her metal companion.

'Next left. One half mile. Hermitage,' said K9 without hesitation. Sarah Jane relaxed a little as the signpost picked out by the lights of the lorry ahead endorsed the robot's map reading. Off the main road the going was slow for the minor roads were minor indeed and, beyond Hermitage, the many branch roads were inadequately signposted. After three miles Sarah Jane and K9 were hopelessly lost.

In the clearing that burgeoned from the footpath through the woods to the east of Bradleigh Manor the double circle had been drawn with white stones and the pentacle formed within. Black-cloaked figures moved silently in the sharp-shadowed light of the moon positioning the altar and driving the tar torches into the frost-hard earth at the four major points of the compass.

'Come on, K9, come on!' cried Sarah Jane. 'What's the matter with you?'

'Imperative have bearing,' responded K9. The clock on the dashboard showed eleven forty-five.

'We're not going to do it!' shouted the tormented girl. 'We're not going to do it!' She saw the isolated telephone box ahead and grasped in agonised desperation at the straw it offered. She had no need to leave the car to see the door to the kiosk was missing, most of the remaining glass was smashed, and the cable to the receiver was hanging loose. Those responsible for repair had obviously retreated in the losing battle with persistent, mindless vandalism. Sarah Jane had run the gamut of intolerable strain and all emotion drained from her. She was empty, cold, resigned, defeated.

'We've lost, K9.'

'Negative, Mistress. Proceed north. Next right turn.'

The irrepressible optimism of the little machine gave her no hope. She went automatically into gear. The dashboard clock showed eleven fifty-five.

Bathed by the full moon and within the ring of fluttering torchlight ten cloaked figures, arranged in symmetrical formation before the altar, stood with upturned faces awaiting the advent of the winter solstice.

K9's inflexible logic had brought its reward. His directions had brought them to a confluence of minor roads and a long sought signpost that pointed to Leigh. The MGB snarled through the hamlet and Sarah Jane brought it to a growling halt to stumble into the ray of hope offered by an undamaged telephone box.

As she dialled 999 she heard a distant church clock begin the sonorous strokes of midnight. When the operator answered Sarah Jane's voice was low and steady, the speech rehearsed: 'Police. Ruined chapel east of Bradleigh Manor, Hazelbury Abbas. Murder. Repeat, Murder. Pass it on!' And she hung up.

A single muted note on a goathorn began a low, moaning chant and Peter Tracey, the insignia of an acolyte worn about his cloak, came into the licking rim light of the torches from behind an overgrown section of ruined wall. He carried a chalice in one hand and the long-handled athame in the other.

He was followed majestically by the High Priest and Priestess garishly caparisoned and anonymous behind the obscene goat masks of their diabolical faith. They took their positions by the altar and Peter Tracey knelt before it. His father's fanatical eyes shifted focus to follow, with pride, the acolyte's movements as he offered the chalice to the High Priestess who, in turn, offered it to the moon.

'O, Almighty Mother of all, Thy humble servant calls upon Thee to bless this cup that is to receive the essence of Thy exhalted purpose.'

Sarah Jane had covered the five miles separating her from the Manor by taking some appalling risks. She turned in at the gates and her tyres spat a fusillade of gravel at the avenue of trees. She rounded the south-east corner of the house, skidding through ninety degrees on the spluttering surface, and thrust the MGB into the mouth of the footpath. Her avid intention was frustrated after fifty yards by the path converging to an impassable width. Leaving the car with the headlights on to light her way, she rushed recklessly along the path indifferent to personal safety.

'Mistress!' called K9.

She stopped and hesitated, doubting the robot could be of any further help.

'Imperative I accompany.'

There was something about the timbre of the robot's voice that made up Sarah Jane's mind. She dashed back to the car.

The High Priestess held the athame high into the light of the moon. 'O, Almighty Mother of all, Thy humble servant calls upon Thee to bless this instrument that will release Thy grand design.'

The chanting began to grow in volume and Sarah Jane heard it with the relief crowded from her mind by terror. She prayed with all her flagging strength that she was not too late. Suddenly K9, who had been keeping pace with her, was no longer there. Barely slackening her speed, she jerked a look over her shoulder. In the slashing rays of moonlight she saw K9 had become entangled with tough tendrils of trailing bramble. 'Wait not!' he called economically.

The chanting built up again as Henry Tobias and Byron Weekes bore Brendan high on the hurdle to the altar. The coven parted to admit the sacrifice to the circle. With devotional care the unconscious boy was lifted from the sacred hurdle to the sacred altar and his ceremonial robe removed to expose his nakedness to the impassible moon. The High Priest stepped nearer the altar with the chalice held ready. The High Priestess slowly raised the athame, the handle clasped in both hands, until her arms were fully extended.

'O, Almighty Mother of all, accept Thou this our unworthy sacrifice,' she chanted and her arms stiffened.

'*No!*' screamed Sarah Jane. 'No, no, no, no, no!'

In the abrupt hush that followed only the trembling hiss of the wind-savaged torches disturbed the utter silence. Sarah Jane was able to continue less stridently.

'Cover him up!' she ordered, pointing shakily at Brendan but managing to keep the tremor from her voice as she called, 'You're finished, the whole evil pack of you. The police are on their way.'

The High Priestess relaxed her taut arms and the coven turned from the intruder to look back towards the altar. A short, insane laugh vibrated from behind the mask of the High Priest. 'She lies! Take her!'

As the coven broke from the circle and advanced, Sarah Jane held her ground. Her leap into a neck kick disposed of one member of the coven and a two-way flailing hand chop dealt with two more before she was overcome. Fighting ferociously, she was borne into the circle and her three paralysed victims dragged into the hallowed area after her. The High Priest pointed at the altar and the chanting recommenced. 'Proceed!' he commanded, and the athame was again raised.

'O, Almighty Mother of all,' repeated the High Priestess, 'accept Thou this our unworthy sacrifice!'

The sacrificial knife was halfway to Brendan's heart when a blinding burst of focused light knocked the High Priestess back from the altar. With a scream of terror the High Priest turned to run but he, too, was cut down. The eight members of the coven remaining upright in the direction of whence the blasts had come.

K9 gleamed brightly in the moonlight at the edge of the

clearing, his eyes blazing and lengths of blaster-burnt bramble still clinging to him. The midwife Creach screamed, 'Hecate!' and ran. K9 cut her down.

The two Traceys took up the cry and, begging for mercy, broke from the circle, only to be despatched by the remorseless robot. As K9 advanced with the relentlessness of a Juggernaut Michael Barnett and Stanley Shields, the publican, who had been holding Sarah Jane, dropped to their knees as did Byron Weekes and two others. The drunken Henry Tobias jumped at Sarah Jane to put her between him and the avenging dog-familiar. She chopped him down with supreme satisfaction. 'Put that in your leader next week!' she said contemptuously.

She ran to the altar to cover the naked Brendan. As she did so she looked across at the insensible bodies of the High Priestess and the High Priest. The goat masks had tumbled from them.

She gazed upon the face of Lily Gregson with astonishment and then with horror on the face of Commander William Pollock.

Sarah Jane fell upon the blissfully unconscious Brendan and wept. Her sobs mingled with the sound of approaching police sirens.

'Operation completed, Mistress,' reported K9.

Epilogue

Brendan sat on a sofa in the Bakers' sitting-room, fully recovered from an ordeal about which he remembered next to nothing, replete with food and not a little drink and the warm satisfaction of being for so long the centre of distinguished attention.

Sarah Jane sat next to him smiling affectionately at the soporific schoolboy smirk. Howard and Juno came back into the room from the hall and the sound of cars pulling away. 'Well, my dears,' purred the successful hostess, 'you're nothing if not a tremendous social hit. I thought they'd never go.'

'And in spite of the embarrassment,' added a hugely amused Howard.

'What embarrassment?' asked Juno with a slight frown.

'Oh, come off it, darling,' smiled her husband. 'Bill Pollock's been the mainstay of Lady Taylor's bridge parties for years.'

'Oh, that,' said Juno, the cloud floating from her face.

Howard took Sarah Jane's empty glass and made a move to replenish it. 'I oughtn't,' said the heroine of Hazelbury Abbas.

'I know you oughtn't,' said her host, 'but you're still twitching after nearly twenty-four hours.'

'Now, be fair to the child,' reprimanded Juno, 'so would you in the circumstances.'

'I'll not deny it,' said Howard, being liberal with the Napoleon brandy. 'There, young lady. I drink to the indelible mark you've made on our community.'

'More like an indelible dent,' grinned Sarah Jane, 'with thirteen of you on a charge of abduction and attempted murder.'

'Not Peter,' said Brendan, 'if I put in a good word for him.'

Sarah Jane laughed suddenly. Juno looked mildly shocked. 'I don't think it's very funny, dear,' she said gently.

'I'm sorry,' said Sarah Jane, 'I was thinking of something else.'

'What, dear?'

'For a while,' admitted the local heroine, 'I thought you and Howard were behind it all.'

Howard's amazement quickly turned to amusement and Juno broke into a merry laugh which stopped just as quickly. 'I don't think that's very funny,' she said.

'Oh, come on, Juno,' said Howard, 'the laugh's on us anyway.'

'What I find funny,' said Brendan unexpectedly and a little sleepily, 'is how they were going to get rid of the body.'

'What body?' asked a startled Juno.

'*My* body?' replied the erstwhile prospective human sacrifice.

'A lime pit,' suggested Howard lightly, 'or a section of motorway.'

'Ghoul!' accused Juno.

'Oh no, not that way at all,' said Brendan. 'I was told on the best authority that what they'd do is make mincemeat out of me and use me as fertiliser.'

'How jolly,' murmured Juno.

'*Whose* best authority?' asked Sarah Jane, her pert nose wrinkled in distaste.

'K9's,' said Brendan happily, adding hastily for the benefit of the Bakers, 'That's the nickname of a friend of mine.'

The ringing of the telephone fortuitously made further explanation unnecessary. Howard excused himself to answer it. 'Hello, Lavinia! How are you? Yes, she is.' He turned to Sarah Jane who was already on her feet and reaching for the receiver.

'Aunt Lavinia?

'Sarah Jane!' The distant voice sounded a little strained. 'I've been ringing home for hours. What are you doing there?'

Sarah Jane's relief and joy were too great for her to be

disturbed by her faraway relation's tone. 'Brendan and I were here for dinner.'

'Well, I wish you'd let me know, dear. It's taken me simply hours to get through to . . .'

'But, Aunt Lavinia, I didn't know where you were.'

'Didn't Bill Pollock tell you? I left word where you could get me.'

Sarah Jane smiled grimly. 'No, he didn't. But why didn't you phone us? We've been so worried about you.'

'Worried? About me? I'm more than capable of looking after myself.'

'Yes, Aunt Lavinia, dear, but you don't know what's been going on here.'

'What's that?'

Sarah Jane turned to smile at the others. 'It'll keep until you get back,' she said. 'And you know that packing case you brought me from Croydon?' – she saw Brendan shake his head slowly – 'That'll keep too.'

A quarter of a mile away in front of a happily burning fire K9 was scanning a sheet of words and music and following the beat with his probe. What sounded like a very flat melody was coming from his speaker: 'While shepherds watched their flocks by night all seated on the ground . . .'